YOU CAN'T HIDE

30 TALES OF TERROR

CHILLING TALES FOR THE CAMPFIRE
BOOK ONE

BLAIR DANIELS

CONTENTS

High Beams	1
Attention Shoppers: Please Hide Immediately	6
I Found A Note I Don't Remember Writing	16
I Think My Husband Is Cheating On Me	22
My Neighbors Have Been Dancing For 5 Hours	29
After My Best Friend Died	32
My Phone Is Taking Strange Photos	44
Wocket In My Pocket	48
My Wife Hates Halloween	54
The Vending Machine	59
My Son Went Missing	67
My Mom's Garden	72
Are You Dreaming Right Now?	84
Wind Phone	90
Christmas Tree Shopping	96
The Sound Only My Wife Can Hear	102
The Bank Deposits	113
My Grandma Is Acting Odd	124
I Left My Recording App On Last Night	129
Matryoshka Doll	133
Water Torture	137
My Basement Fell Into An Abandoned Mine	145
The Uncanny Valley	154
My Roommate Is Trying To Kill Me	166
I Accidentally Summoned Stan Instead Of Satan	172
I See People Hiding Their Faces	181
My Husband Makes Me Wear A Wig	194

Footprints In The Snow	204
The Scariest Board Game	214
There's Something Imitating My Son	229

HIGH BEAMS

It first happened around Wilhelmina Drive.

When the sedan passed me, it flashed its high beams. A cop was ahead, or even more likely—deer. I hit the brakes, scanning the forest on either side.

But nothing popped up. No cop hidden on the side of the road, ready to pounce on speeders. No herd of deer staring at me with glowing eyes in the darkness. And I'd definitely turned off my own brights as soon as the other car came into view.

When I'd gotten about a mile away, I figured it was safe. I pushed my foot on the accelerator and resumed my usual speed. *Must've been a herd of deer that crossed already.*

I turned up the radio, a staticky *Carry on My Wayward Son* coming through. Damn, the reception in the valley really sucked. But my phone's battery was low, and I wasn't about to use up all the juice playing *Every Rose Has Its Thorn* for the 100th time.

I turned the dial, but the rest of the stations seemed even more staticky. *At least I'll be home soon.*

I was halfway through making a mental checklist of everything I had to get done tomorrow, when another pair of headlights blinked through the trees.

When it got about twenty feet from me—

It flashed its high beams, too.

More deer?

But as I drove through the darkness... I didn't see anything. No cop cars, either, unless they were really well hidden. As the seconds ticked by and there was nothing else—no construction zone, tree in the road, or other hazard—my heart began to pound.

What was he trying to warn me about?

I glanced down at my phone, the screen black in the passenger seat. *Is it already dead?* Maybe they were warning me about something wrong with my car. Both headlights seemed to be working, but maybe there was smoke coming out of my tailpipe, or something.

I didn't like the idea of being stuck on the side of the road at 11 PM.

I sucked in a deep breath. *It's probably just deer. There are lots of them around here, remember?* The green sign for EDGAR AVE. popped up in my headlights, and my heart slowed. *Less than ten minutes from home.*

I thought of the fluffy, furry blanket I'd just gotten a week ago. Curling up in it, eating some chocolate before bed as Leela snuggled up next to me. The thought made my heart slow even further. My cat, my room, my blanket...

Another pair of headlights swung around the bend.

As it approached me, it slowed.

And then it flashed its high beams at me.

My blood went cold.

For some reason, two flashes seemed to fit within the realm of coincidence. But three… *It's not deer or a cop. It's something about **me**.* Something wrong with the car, or—

A horrible thought shot through my mind.

That urban legend. Where a girl's driving home late, and a truck keeps following her and flashing his high beams. But the trucker is a nice dude, and he's flashing the headlights because there's a guy in the backseat with a knife and he keeps rising up to stab her—

Oh God oh God—

I turned on the lights and whipped around.

The backseat was empty.

At least, as far as I could tell. Swinging my gaze back to the road, I reached my hand around the back of my seat.

My heart pounded in my chest as I slowly, *slowly* swept my fingers through the darkness behind me. *What if there's someone there?* I imagined my fingers meeting rough cloth. Warm skin. Sticky hot breath. The cold steel point of a knife.

But they only met air.

I breathed a sigh of relief. Swished my hand through the air a few more times, high and low. There was a dead spot that I couldn't reach, but it would be far too small for an adult man to hide in. Unless he was some kind of gold medal contortionist.

So maybe it's something wrong with the car then. Maybe

they see smoke, or a door's ajar, or a light's out... I glanced at the side of the road. There was a margin of dirt between the edge of the road and the beginning of the forest; I could safely pull over and check what was wrong.

Then again, this road was really lonely. Especially so late. There were only a few houses on this road, and none that I could see right now. Just thick woods, brambles and twisted bark that would muffle any screams...

I'll take my chances driving home.

I gripped the steering wheel. *Only about five more miles.* I again thought of my warm little house, and Leela, with her fluffy black fur and permanent smirk...

A pickup truck swung around the bend. I held my breath. *They're not flashing at me. Good. Good. Almost home—*

But then, there it was.

Flash.

The afterimage of the searing white light danced in my vision. Cold sweat broke out on my neck. "Dammit," I whispered. "What the *hell* is going on?!"

Their headlights disappeared behind me—and the darkness immediately pooled around me again, like fluid filling a void. Scraggly, crooked branches clawed at my car, silhouetted by the full moon. The radio played straight static. I reached for my phone—

And then I heard it.

Tap, tap, tap

Coming from straight above me.

Something was tapping on my moonroof.

My entire body shook. The dark road in front of me

became a blur. *No. This can't be happening. How could someone even be...* I jammed my foot on the accelerator. The speedometer shot to 30, 35, 40...

Tap, tap, tap.

Without looking up, I reached a shaking hand up to the moonroof. I pressed my hand against the glass. It felt *warm*. Even though it was only 40 degrees outside.

Fuck oh what the fuck—

I couldn't look up. It was just this visceral instinct. Like the feeling you get when you know someone is watching you, and your brain is screaming *hide*. I bit my lip, staring at the road, waiting for my street to come up.

Tap, tap, tap.

Don't look up. Don't look up. Don't look up.

MAPLE WOODS appeared before me. I swung onto the street, then pulled into the driveway. Without even thinking it through, I swung the door open and ran as fast as I possibly could.

Surprisingly, I got inside safe and sound.

I spent half the night watching old movies, Leela curled on my lap. I checked the front and back doors, and all the windows, about a million times each. I didn't dare look outside at my car. I closed my eyes, even, when checking the front door.

I thought I was safe.

But I wasn't.

Because now, I hear it again. *Tap-tap-tap.* It's more frequent now, more frantic. Coming from right above me. Right above my bed.

Coming from inside my attic.

ATTENTION SHOPPERS: PLEASE HIDE IMMEDIATELY

"**Attention shoppers,**" came a male voice over the intercom. "**Please move to the back of the store immediately.**"

"The back of the store?" I whispered to Daniel. "Don't they mean the front of the store? To pay for our stuff?"

It was 8:50 pm – 10 minutes till closing time. We'd brought our two kids out on this late-night Walmart excursion in the hopes of burning off some energy; instead, they'd just thrown tantrums for new Legos and Hot Wheels. It was a disaster.

But apparently, the disaster was just beginning.

"**Please move to the back of the store immediately,**" the voice repeated overhead. "**This is not a drill.**"

I glanced around—but the other shoppers were just as confused as I was. An old lady looked up at the ceiling, scrunching her face. "What the hell?" a dark-haired woman asked her boyfriend, pushing a cart full of garden supplies.

"Didn't you hear?" an older man said, leaning over his cart of bottled water and canned food. "We're in a tornado watch. One touched down in Sauerville."

A tornado? It was definitely storming outside. I'd seen the black clouds roll in from the east earlier. But it didn't look *that* bad.

"Do not stay out in the open. I repeat—do NOT stay out in the open."

There was a pause. Then, an explosion of sound, as everyone began to mobilize. Carts rolling, panicked voices, feet slapping on the floor.

No. No no no. This can't be happening...

I hurried down the toy aisle, Tucker in my arms, Daniel and Jackson following me. Three zig-zaggy turns, and then we were in the electronics area. I glanced at the TVs on the wall—

And pictured the four of us, crushed underneath them.

"Stay away from windows and doors," the voice continued on the loudspeaker. **"And do NOT attempt to exit the store."**

"Is this—is it safe here?"

Daniel shook his head. "Big open areas aren't good. I'm going to check in back, see if there's a break room or something. You stay here, okay?"

I nodded.

Arms shaking, I sat down on the ground between two shelves of video games. Tucker sucked on a bottle in my arms while Jackson began to giggle. "Is the tornado going to hit the store? And everything will fly around, real fast?" he asked with a big stupid grin on his face.

"I don't know."

A tornado. A real-life tornado, like you see in the movies, plowing through our town. It was so... unfathomable. We were New York natives, transplanted here to Indiana only six months ago. I'd never been in a tornado watch my entire life.

Daniel jogged back into view. "Everything's locked up," he said, as he joined me on the floor. "But listen. Fairview's a big town. The chances that it'll hit *this* Walmart... I think we'll be okay."

"I never should've brought us here."

"You didn't know. None of us did." He wrapped his arm around me. "They should've warned us. Like an emergency alert on our phones. Or a tornado siren, or something."

The voice overhead rang out again through the store.

"Do not stay out in the open. Do not make yourself visible. That includes security cameras—please move to a spot that is not visible to any cameras."

I frowned. "What does that have to do with tornadoes?"

A feeling of unease, in the pit of my stomach. I glanced up, and saw several black globes descending from the ceiling, hiding the cameras within.

"I guess we should listen to them and get out of sight," I whispered.

I grabbed Jackson's hand, Daniel picked up Tucker, and we jogged out into the center aisle. The store was an eerie sight—abandoned shopping carts, askew in the aisle, full of everything from pies to batteries to plants. Footsteps echoed around the store from people unseen, as they found their new hiding places.

We dodged a shopping cart full of soda, ran through kitchenwares, and then stopped in the Easter decoration aisle. There was a camera in the central corridor, but as long as we stayed in the middle of Easter aisle, we'd be invisible.

The four of us crouched on the floor, next to some demented-looking Easter bunnies. "I'm hungry," Jackson whined.

"*Sssshhh.*"

"Mommy—"

I grabbed a bag of colorful chocolate eggs and ripped it open. "Here. Candy. Happy?" I whispered, thrusting them into his hands. Then I leaned back against the metal shelves, panting.

But I didn't have long to rest. A mechanical whine overhead, and then the voice came through the speakers again.

"Keep away from aisles with food. If you have food with you, leave it and move to a new hiding place. If you have any open wounds, cover them with clothing."

What... the fuck?

That had *nothing* to do with keeping safe in a tornado.

"We should make a run for it," Daniel whispered to me, starting to stand.

"But... the tornado—"

"I don't think there *is* a tornado. Listen. Do you hear any wind?"

I listened. But all I heard was silence. No howling wind, no shaking ground, no projectiles clanging against the metal roof.

"Maybe... maybe it's still coming. I know what they're saying doesn't make sense but to go *outside*—"

"We need to get out of here. *Now*." He grabbed Jackson's hand as he held Tucker in his arms. "Come on."

"Daniel, I don't think that's a good idea," I whispered.

But the next words from the intercom changed my mind.

"Assume a fetal position and place your hands on your head. Close your eyes and do not open them for any reason."

"Let's go."

We broke into a sprint and ran down the central aisle, cameras be damned. The front door appeared in front of us—a little black rectangle looming in the distance.

And as we got closer, I saw Daniel was right.

There was a tree at the border of the parking lot, under a streetlamp.

It was perfectly still.

We continued running, past the clothing area, past the snacks lined up at the checkout lines. I ran towards the sliding glass doors as fast as my legs would carry me. *Almost there. Almost there. Almost—*

The doors didn't open.

"No. No, no, no."

Daniel slammed his body against the door. It rattled underneath him. I tried to squeeze my fingers into the gap between them, to try and pull them apart.

They didn't budge.

"They... they locked us in," I whispered.

"I want to go home," Jackson said. Tucker was beginning to fuss too, making little noises like he was about to start full-on wailing.

I turned around—

And that's when I saw him.

A Walmart employee.

He was sitting on the ground at the end of one of the checkout aisles. Facing away from us. Wearing the familiar blue vest with a golden starburst.

"Hey! Let us out!"

He didn't reply.

"Did you hear me? I don't care if there's a fucking tornado. Unlock the door and let us out!"

Again, he said nothing.

But in the silence, I could hear something. A wet, smacking sound. I stared at the man, slightly hunched over, still facing away from me.

Was he... *eating*... something?

The speaker overhead crackled to life.

"**Attention. Please do NOT talk to any Walmart employees.**"

My blood ran cold.

The smacking sound stopped. And then, slowly, the man began to stand. He placed his palms on the conveyor belt and pushed up—and I could see that they were stained with blood. I backed away—but my legs felt like they were moving through a vat of honey.

No, no, no—

Fingers locked around my arm and yanked.

"Come on!" Daniel shouted.

I sprinted after him, deeper into the store. Tucker stared at me over his shoulder, and Jackson ran as fast as his little feet would take him. I was vaguely aware of the *slap-slap-slap* sound behind me, but I didn't dare look back.

Daniel ran into the clothing area and I swayed, dodging circular racks of T-shirts and wooden displays of baby clothes. He skidded to a stop and ducked into the dressing room area. "In here!" he whispered, motioning at one of the rooms.

We piled inside and locked the door.

"Daddy," Jackson started.

"You listen to me *very carefully,*" I said, crouching to his level. "You have to be absolutely silent. Do not say a *word.* Okay?"

Jackson looked at me, then Daniel—then he nodded and sat down on the floor.

"I'm going to try to call 911," Daniel whispered, transferring Tucker to me and pulling out his phone. He tapped at the screen—then frowned.

"What?"

"We don't... we don't seem to have any service. I don't—"

Thump.

I grabbed Jackson and pulled him away from the door. The four of us huddled in the corner. I held my breath.

Thump.

Under the gap of the dressing room door—men's feet in black shoes. They slowly took a step forward, deeper into the dressing room.

"Don't... move," I whispered, holding Jackson.

The man took another step.

Don't make a sound. Don't move. Don't—

Tucker let out a soft cry.

The man stopped. His feet turned, pointing at us. *No. No, no, no.* Tucker let out another cry—louder this time. My nails dug into Daniel's hand. *No—*

A hand appeared. It slowly pressed against the floor, stained with blood. And then his knees appeared, as he lowered himself down to the gap.

No.

Could he fit under? The gap wasn't small—it was like the stall door to a bathroom. If he flattened himself against the floor... there's a chance he could fit under.

I watched in horror as his stomach came into view. His blue Walmart vest, as he lowered his body to the floor. Then he pushed his arm under the gap and blindly swept it across the floor.

As if feeling for us.

This is it. We're going to die.

And then he lowered his head.

His face. Oh, God, there was something horribly wrong with his face. He smiled up at us with a smile that was impossibly wide, showing off blood-stained teeth. His skin was so pale it was nearly blue. And his eyes... they were milky white, without pupils or irises.

I opened my mouth to scream—

"Attention shoppers," the voice began overhead.

No no no—

"Please make your way to the front of the store and make your final purchases. We will be closing in ten minutes."

... What?

And then—before I could react—something unseen jerked the man out of view.

A strange dragging sound followed. As if someone was dragging his body out of the dressing room area. I stared at the door, shaking, as Tucker's cries rang in my ears.

But he didn't come back.

And within ten minutes, the usual hubbub of Walmart returned. Voices. Footsteps. Shopping cart wheels rolling along the floor.

Shaking, I finally got up and unlocked the door.

The store looked completely normal. People were lined up at the cash registers, placing their goods on the conveyor belts. Employees were scanning tags, printing receipts. People walked towards the glass doors, and when they did—they slid open.

As we slowly walked towards the exit, I spotted the older man who'd warned us about the tornado earlier.

"What—what *was* that?" I asked, unable to keep my voice from shaking.

He shrugged. "I guess the tornado missed us! What a miracle, huh?"

Giving us a smile, he disappeared out the glass doors and into the night.

I FOUND A NOTE I DON'T REMEMBER WRITING

It was taped to the bathroom mirror. At my eye level, covering up my reflection. Five words.

Don't look under the bed.

I peeled it off the mirror and looked down at it. It was in my handwriting—my sloppy, chicken-scratch handwriting. More sloppy than usual, like I'd been in a rush writing it. I turned it over in my hands, confused.

Don't look under the bed?

I didn't remember writing it. At all. *Maybe I wrote it when I was half-asleep?* Weird.

I walked back into the bedroom. Nothing looked amiss—just my blue-gray comforter, bunched up on one side. My pillow askew. A cup of water and my phone on the nightstand.

I began to crouch down—

Arf! Arf!

I ran down the stairs to find Sadie, scratching at the

back door. "You need to go out, huh?" I glanced up at the clock—12:23 PM.

How did I sleep so late?

I let her out, then headed towards the kitchen. But as I got closer, the sour smell of decay hit my nostrils.

Oh, no—

My heart stopped as I stepped in.

Red. Red everywhere. Splattered up the sides of the cabinets. Pooling across the floor. I sucked in a breath to scream—

And then spotted the jar of marinara.

It was shattered in the middle of the floor. Red sauce splattered in every direction from that central point, covering half the kitchen. And as I looked around, there was the source of the smell: an opened package of ground beef on the counter. Beside it sat a half-diced onion on the cutting board, a teaspoon full of kosher salt. Two wine glasses—one half-drunk—sat on the kitchen table, along with my wallet and keys.

Did I have Henry over last night...?

Arf!

Sadie's bark tore me from my thoughts. I let her in and then collapsed on the couch. "What happened last night?" I muttered.

Maybe I hit my head? Maybe I dropped the marinara sauce, slipped in it, and hit my head on the floor. Got a concussion, went up to my bedroom, and fell asleep. But then wouldn't there be sauce in the bed?

I sighed and pulled out my phone. I'd give my boyfriend Henry a call and see if he remembered anything. But as soon as I unlocked my phone, I saw the notification.

1 New Voicemail

A chill ran down my spine. I called into the voicemail service and waited, chewing on my lip—

"Listen. *Listen to me.*"

My blood ran cold. It was *my* voice.

"As soon as you get up, get out of the house. Take Sadie and get out. And whatever you do—do *not* look under the bed."

That was it. That was the whole message.

A powerful feeling of derealization hit me. You probably know the feeling I'm talking about: that nothing is real, my entire life has been a dream, no one exists but me. It's usually just an intrusive thought... but now I felt like it was grabbing me by the shoulders and shaking me.

I don't remember anything.

Is this even real?

Am I dreaming?

I forced myself off that train of thought and dialed Henry's number. The phone rang once, twice, three times...

It went to voicemail.

"Why aren't you picking up?" I growled into the phone. "The one time I need you..." That was just like Henry. I slipped the phone back into my pocket and stared at Sadie. She stared back at me with her big, brown eyes.

Get out of the house. Do not look under the bed.

I forced myself up off the couch. "Okay, we're going

to the dog park!" Sadie sped by me like a bullet. Hands shaking, I grabbed my laptop, a few other necessities, and shoved them into my bag. I pulled the strap over my shoulder, dialed Henry one more time, and prayed for him to pick up—

No.

There was a sound from upstairs.

The sound of a ringing phone.

Every muscle in my body froze. With shaking hands, I pressed the red "end call" button on my phone. A second later, the ringing ceased.

Oh, God...

No, no, no...

I stepped onto the first stair. The old wood creaked underneath me. I took another step, then another, until I was standing motionless in the hallway.

Don't look under the bed.

I stepped forward. My hands shook as I reached for the doorknob. Twisted it, pulled it open.

I stepped in the room. It looked as it always had. The same comforter, the same items on the nightstand. Everything the same. My gaze flicked to the dark shadows underneath the bed. With shaking hands, I pulled out my phone and dialed Henry again. *Please don't ring. Please don't—*

It rang from under the bed.

My throat went dry. I slowly crouched down, my entire body shaking like a leaf. My heart pounded as my hands splayed against the carpet, balancing myself. *Please, no. No, no no—*

It was him.

His skin was pale, almost blue. The mattress pressed into his tall frame, as if he'd been shoved and kicked under there until he fit. And his eyes... his eyes were empty and lifeless, boring into me as though he knew what I'd done.

I ran over to the bathroom and puked. Wiped my face off, gripped the bathroom sink to keep myself from fainting.

Did... did I kill him?

The half-drunk wine glass. *Did I poison him?*

That had to be it. There was no blood. *But why? Why did I do it? What happened last night? What—*

Arf!

Sadie's bark was like a shock of cold water.

I have to get out of here.

I ran down the stairs. She was pawing at the front door. "Just—just a second," I said, as I stumbled back towards the kitchen. "I need to get the keys."

I ran back into the kitchen. I carefully stepped around the shards of broken glass, the splatters of tomato sauce. I reached out for the keys—

And then something hit me.

Not quite a memory--more of an intuition, a gut feeling. Like the memory was poking up from my subconscious, about to break the surface.

The salt.

I ran over to the teaspoon of salt lying on the counter, next to the cutting board. Slowly bent over so that it was eye level.

It wasn't salt.

I could see that now. It wasn't the coarse, irregular

flakes of kosher salt I kept in a pig by the stove--it was a fine powder.

And it smelled terrible.

The memory hit me like a truck. Getting out of the shower. Putting on a vampy lipstick. Poking my head into the kitchen while Henry was making dinner for our one-month anniversary.

Stopping dead as he swirled white powder into the wine glass.

Backing up. Mind reeling. Almost fainting. Stumbling forward and hearing him call out my name.

Carrie? You there?

I walked in, pretending I didn't see anything.

And he bought it.

I knew that the glass of wine he offered me with a smile had something in it. Whether it was a date rape drug or poison, I didn't know. But I did know this. If I let on that I knew—if I tried to call the police—I might not make it out of there alive.

So when he turned to finish chopping the onion, I switched the glasses.

I wavered in the kitchen, black dots dancing in my vision. Then I sucked in a breath and walked to the front door, where Sadie stood waiting for me.

"Come on," I said, as I opened the door. "Let's go."

I THINK MY HUSBAND IS CHEATING ON ME

I knew it when I found the hair.

While changing the bedsheets, I found a long, black hair. Curled up right next to my husband's pillow. There's no way it could be mine—I'm blonde.

"Any idea who this is from?" I demanded, shoving the hair in his face.

"What is that? A hair?"

"I found it *in our bed*."

He looked from me to the hair, then back again. "Are you saying... you think I'm cheating on you?"

Of course that's what I'm saying, I wanted to shout. *There's another woman's hair in our bed!* But I swallowed, stepped back, and took a deep breath instead. "Do you know whose hair this is?"

"No idea. Maybe from Tanya, when she visited?"

I mean, to be fair, Greg's never given me any reason to think he's cheating. He's a computer nerd who spends most of his time on Reddit or playing D&D. He's attractive, but not an Adonis by any standard. I haven't noticed any missing time, and he doesn't seem overly protective of his phone.

But the clues kept piling up.

For one, I started finding the hairs *everywhere*. One on the kitchen counter. Another in my home office. A few on our couch. When I emptied our Roomba, there were a dozen or more, all tangled up with the dust.

One night, I smelled perfume. Greg claimed he couldn't smell it. How could he not? It was really unique. Sweet and floral, yet with a tangy undertone. Almost sour.

Smelling it made my stomach turn.

Another night I went into the bathroom, and saw something small and red on the tile. Like a shard of plastic, maybe, that had broken off something. I bent down and picked it up—only to find that it looked like a fingernail. Yellowish-white on one side, red lacquer on the other.

But it was so small, I really couldn't be sure.

Little incidents like this kept happening every few weeks. A hair, a whiff of perfume. Every time I almost had a panic attack. Sometimes I'd confront Greg in a wild rage; other times, I'd just innocently ask him what it was. It depended on my mood. How desperate I was feeling.

He continued denying it. And I really, truly, started to believe him. I told myself that it was all in my head. I was being paranoid. My marriage was fine.

But then I found the smoking gun.

On Saturday, I was supposed to go out to dinner

with a friend. But as soon as I got to the restaurant, I got a text from her, saying she had to cancel. Disappointed, when I got home I went straight up to the bathroom and started a nice, hot shower going. I peeled off my clothes, waited for clouds of steam to pour out, and then threw back the shower curtain.

There was something in the drain.

I bent over to inspect it—and my blood ran cold.

It was a clump of black hair.

"How do you explain this?!" I yelled, running out of the bathroom naked. I dropped the wet clump of hair on his chest.

He stared at me, at a loss for words. "Uh... what?"

"Her hair was in the shower!"

"Whose hair?" he asked, picking the clump off his shirt and grimacing.

"Don't you fucking gaslight me. Your *girlfriend's* hair!"

"Haley..." He looked into my eyes, and he really did seem honest, in that moment. "I really don't know whose hair this is. But I'm not cheating on you."

"How stupid do you think I am?" I growled, like a rabid animal. "There. Is. Another. Woman's. Hair. In. Our. Shower!"

"Okay, you need to calm down." He threw the hair on the nightstand, stood up, and gently wrapped his hands around my shoulders. "I understand why you would think I'm cheating. But I'm not. I promise—"

"She's in the closet, isn't she?"

"What?"

I looked down at the trail of water on the carpet. Leading straight from the bathroom to the closet.

"That's just from me. I just took a shower, and went to the closet to get my clothes."

I sidestepped him. "Haley," he said in a warning voice behind me, but I didn't listen. I ran across the room, grabbed the double doors, and slid them back.

It was empty.

I pushed our shirts back. Kicked the piles of laundry on the floor. Even went on my tiptoes and checked the high shelf.

Nothing.

"I told you I wasn't having an affair."

This doesn't prove anything, I wanted to yell. *So she's not here. It still doesn't explain the hair, the perfume, or any of the other fuckery going on in our house.*

But I forced myself to shut up. Because no matter what I said, if he were having an affair, he wouldn't tell me.

I'd have to find out on my own.

The next day I left for my mom's.

I left before he woke up. With everything going on, I just couldn't face him. I needed space. Time alone. I sent him a text after I got there, telling him I'd be home in three days.

But I just missed him too much—so I came back after two.

I drove home in silence, my knuckles white on the

steering wheel, my heart pounding in my chest. I pulled into the driveway near midnight. The house was dark, except for the dim night light we always left on in the bathroom.

I quietly slid the key into the lock and opened the door.

The house looked just like it did when I left. Dirty dishes piled up by the sink and a clump of laundry sat in the corner. I walked over to the stairs, trying to be as quiet as possible.

And then I heard it.

Light, thumping footsteps—coming from right above me.

My heart dropped.

I ran up the stairs, taking them two at a time. *No, no, no.* I raced down the hallway, our door looming at the end. *It can't be. It can't—*

I burst into the bedroom.

The adrenaline rushed out of me as I realized... it was empty.

Well, Greg was there. In bed, asleep—or pretending to be. But the room was dark and silent, and everything looked as it should.

Did I imagine the footsteps? No. There was no way. I scanned the room, slowly, looking for anything out of place—

My eyes caught on the closet.

No.

Sticking out from the slats was a lock of black hair.

My blood ran cold. I took a step forward, my heart

hammering in my chest. "Greg, I know you're not asleep," I said softly, not taking my eyes off the door.

He didn't stir.

"You're playing some sick kind of game, Greg, you know that?" I whispered, my eyes locked on the black hair. "Come out, *now,*" I said, my voice shaking. "Or you'll be sorry."

A faint thumping sound in reply.

I ran over to the closet doors. My hands locked on the handles. I sucked in a breath—

"Haley?"

Greg was slowly sitting up in bed, rubbing his eyes. "What are you doing back so early?"

I turned to him. He looked terrible—like he hadn't slept in days. Eyes red and swollen, deep circles underneath.

I let go of the doors and backed away. He reached for me, but I kept going, until my feet hit the cold tile of the bathroom. I grabbed the door and shut it in his face. Clicked the lock.

The bathroom was dark, only lit by the nightlight. My panicked breaths echoed against the walls. I wrapped my arms around myself and began to sob.

There's no way that could be my husband's mistress.

Because she was dead.

The night I found the hair in the drain, I snapped. I stole Greg's phone and eventually found the secret stash of texts. A quick Google search found her address. I went over there at 4 AM, raging with fury, and ended the only threat to my marriage.

Then I went to my mom's house, because I couldn't face him. Came back after two days, because I missed him.

But I never should have come back.

A soft sound jolted me from my thoughts. A wet *squelch*.

My head snapped to the bathtub.

There was a dark shape behind the shower curtain. Shifting, slowly, as more wet *smacks* echoed against the walls.

I reached for the light switch.

Bright light flooded the small room. I squinted, wiping the tears from my eyes, and then glanced at the bathtub. Nothing there.

But when I pulled back the curtain, there was a clump of black hair in the drain.

MY NEIGHBORS HAVE BEEN DANCING FOR 5 HOURS

"I think the Seymours are having a party."

I could see them clearly through our kitchen window. Gabby and Clayton in their dimly-lit family room, dancing. The whole nine yards: waving arms, gyrating hips, clapping hands, stomping feet. Rhythmically moving to the faint bass notes that cut through the summer air.

"At least the music isn't loud," Shirley replied. "Are you sure it's a party? There's no one else parked in their driveway."

Now that she mentioned it, I realized I didn't see anyone else through the windows. Just Gabby and Clayton. I watched as they joined for a second—locking hands, dancing around a central point like two planets orbiting a star, and then breaking free into wild swaying.

"Huh. I guess they're just... dancing by themselves?"

"It's good exercise. Like Zumba," she replied.

"But it's almost 9 o'clock. Kind of late to be exercising."

She shrugged, stirring her spoon around in her chamomile tea.

I finally tore my eyes from the window. With a sigh, I heaved myself out of the chair and started up the stairs, my creaky old joints popping with every step.

Something woke me up.

I glanced at my phone—1:17 AM. Groaning, I rolled out of bed and made my way over to the bathroom.

The Seymours were still dancing.

I could see their small silhouettes below, dancing with the same level of energy they had been four hours ago. Thrashing their arms and gyrating their hips, side-stepping through the room and clapping their hands.

"Where do they get all that energy?" I whispered to myself, watching in amazement through the bathroom window. "Drugs. It must be drugs," I decided.

I watched them, hypnotized. They stepped across the room, swaying their hips, then shimmying. When they passed each other, they reached their arms out, and again locked hands. For several seconds they spun around each other, arms locked, like Rose and Jack in the *Titanic*.

I shrugged and made my way back to bed.

2:27 AM.

I woke with a start this time. Heart pounding in my chest, gasping for air. I grabbed the glass of water on my nightstand and downed half of it.

As I sat there, trying to remember the nightmare that had scared me awake, I heard it.

A rustling sound in the grass.

Something was outside.

Probably just a deer. Or one of those bears that's been breaking into everyone's garbage. I ran over to the window and peeled back the curtain.

What the...

Clayton and Gabby were *in our backyard*.

And they were still dancing. Arms waving, feet kicking, gyrating and swaying to some beat I couldn't hear.

Then they danced forward. Into the light from our back porch. And I saw their faces for the first time.

They were both smiling.

Clayton's face was twisted into a manic, frenzied grin. A grin wider than I've ever seen him smile. Watery mascara streamed down Gabby's cheeks as she grinned, too. Crying with joy.

I leapt back from the window.

And that's where I am now. Locked in the master bedroom with Shirley, sitting on the bed, typing this out. I thought they'd go away. But they're not. They're just dancing, slowly but surely, towards our back door.

In a second I'm going to wake Shirley and call the police. I really am. But... well, there's a problem.

I can't stop my foot from tapping on the carpet.

Tapping to some unheard beat.

AFTER MY BEST FRIEND DIED

It was the beginning of June. That night, the moon was full. Bright silver moonlight shone across the rippling water. But here, under the bridge, it was still dark. I could barely see Tina's green eyes against the shadows.

"We're going to be seniors next year," she said. In a sad, somber tone of voice I'd never heard her use before. "Promise me, no matter where we end up, we won't grow apart. Promise me we'll be friends—forever."

We were sitting at our usual hangout spot. In the woods behind Tina's house, under the concrete bridge that spanned across the creek. We sat on the ledge, feet dangling in the air as the water rushed and murmured below us.

"Of course I promise! Wherever we are, I'll be texting you every day. You'll be annoyed with me, it'll be so much."

She didn't smile.

"Tina?"

"Let's promise to meet right here, every year."

My brows furrowed. "What do you mean?"

"I mean, we make a pact. That every, say... July 12th, at midnight, we meet here."

"Uh... okay... but we'll see each other a lot more than once a year. Even if we're thousands of miles away."

"Just promise me, Madhu."

I thought I could make out the glint of tears in her eyes.

"Uh, sure, I promise."

She reached into her bag. I heard the sound of a zipper—then a wet *smack* as she rubbed something on her hand. *What is she—*

She grabbed my hand and shook it.

"Ew, Tina! What *is* that?"

"Just trying to make our pact permanent. Like a blood pact."

"What..."

"I'm just kidding! It's new lotion I got at Target. Sniff it. Vanilla and cinnamon."

I sniffed. It did smell like vanilla and cinnamon—though there was a hint of something else, too. Something sort of earthy. "I don't like it," I said as I wiped the gunk off on my jeans. "Next time you put lotion on me, could you, like, *warn* me first?"

She giggled.

And so, a tradition was born. Around 11:30pm every July 11th, I'd pack up a small stash of my parents' alcohol and bring it down to the stream. Tina would be waiting for me—somehow, she always got there first—and we'd drink whiskeyed-up root beers while splashing our feet in the cool water, talking about everything under the sun.

Finally, July 12th, 2019 came. The summer after senior year. I was going off to the east coast for NYU, while Tina was going to college just an hour over the Indiana state border.

That meeting had a different vibe. She was quiet as I climbed down the riverbank. As I walked towards her, cool water running over my bare toes, and then pulled myself up onto the ledge.

"So. We're going to be more than a thousand miles away," Tina said.

"Yep," I replied.

We drank our whiskey-root-beers in silence for a few minutes.

"Promise me you'll meet me here next year."

"You know I will."

I didn't tell her that night. I wanted to—badly—but the timing just wasn't right. We were going to be a thousand miles apart. Attending different colleges. Leading different lives, so far away from everything that we had ever known.

I couldn't tell her my secret, no matter how desperately I wanted to.

So I pressed my lips together and acted normal. Talked about everything we always talked about. Tina's sister was still overprotective, telling her not to drink at college (oops, too late) and that we were probably going to get murdered if we kept hanging out at the creek in the middle of the night. Anthony was still a good-for-nothing cheater, cheating on his new girlfriend only two months after he broke up with me.

For three hours, I felt like things were normal, like nothing was changing. Like everything was going to be the same.

Forever.

Around three am, we snuck back through the woods and went home. I saw Tina a few more times that summer—in the daylight, in coffee shops and ice cream parlors, never at the old creek where there was nothing between us but the murmuring water. Then I was waving goodbye and hopping on a plane to New York City.

And I hate to say it... but Tina was right.

Between classes and social events, I didn't have much time for friends back home. Even Tina. Daily texting sessions, telling each other every minute detail of our days, slowly turned to once-a-week "how are you"s. Tina wanted to visit me—she brought it up a few times, offering to meet halfway or even drive all the way up to New York. But somehow the dates never lined up. Somehow there just wasn't the time between quizzes and parties and new friends.

And then it happened.

I was on the way back from Biochem when I got the call. "Madhu, I'm so, so sorry," my mom said, barely understandable through sobs. "But Tina's dad just told me, she got in a car accident..."

No. The student center spun around me as I stood, locked in place, praying she wasn't going to say those next four words.

"She didn't make it."

The next few weeks were a blur as I flew home to attend Tina's funeral. As I stood up and said words about my best friend in the whole world. Tina's dad, normally stoic and gruff, bawled his eyes out in the front row. Her sister Tiffany, sharing Tina's tall build and curly hair, just stared at me with hollow eyes.

I didn't blame her. I felt hollow too, like a piece of me was just... gone.

And I didn't even get to tell her...

That summer I got an internship in Dayton, only an hour from my childhood home. As July 11th approached, I got increasingly depressed. I had to take a few sick days off work just to get my head on straight.

After a long therapy session, I decided to go down to the old bridge on July 12th. I'd drink a whiskey root beer and celebrate her life. Tell her all the times she made me smile. Maybe her ghost would hear me and smile too.

And I'd finally tell her my secret.

Tina's dad didn't live there anymore, but I snuck through the backyard anyway, keeping to the edge of the woods. It was hard seeing her bicycle gone, replaced by a little toy car for toddlers. I swallowed down the tears and entered the woods, the liquor bag heavy on my shoulders.

It was a hot, sticky July night. Crickets chirped as I made my way through the woods, the leaves crunching under my feet.

And then I heard the gurgles of the stream.

I angled my body as I climbed down the muddy

riverbank. I toed off my shoes, left them on one of the low rocks by the shore, and stepped into the water.

The darkness under the bridge was impenetrable. I set my bag on the ledge, hoisted myself up. Popped open a can of root beer, took a sip. Poured whiskey out of the flask until the can was overflowing.

Then I finally spoke.

"So. Tina. You didn't show."

I forced a laugh—but it came out as more of a strangled sob.

"Fuck, I wish you were here right now. I miss you so much."

I took a sip. Then another. And another.

"Remember that time in third grade? When you threw up on Jenna Bartley on front of Seth? She was soooo pissed. Every time we passed her in the hallway she looked like she wanted to strangle you."

Only the soft gurgles of the stream replied.

"Yeah. We had some good times, didn't we?" I took a long sip. The crickets had stopped chirping—or maybe they'd never been chirping in the forest, only in the neighborhood. I didn't remember.

"There was something I never got to tell you." I swallowed, the lump in my throat growing. "I meant to. But I was scared. And I kept waiting, and waiting..."

I sucked in a deep breath. I knew I was just talking to thin air, but my heart was pounding in my chest. *Just say it.* My hands trembled.

"Tina, I... I think I was in love with you."

The water gently lapped over the rocks.

"I don't know. But the way I felt about you, it was

different from the way I felt about anyone else. Even Anthony. The night he broke up with me, I was bawling my eyes out, but... somehow I knew it was all going to be okay. Because I had you."

I took a sip straight from the flask.

"I didn't want to say anything because I didn't want to ruin our friendship. And I wasn't even sure if that's what it was, you know? I mean, I don't like girls. But... I liked *you*."

A tear rolled down my cheek.

"I *loved* you."

And then I heard it.

A soft *snap*.

I jolted upright. Then I sucked in a deep breath. *Calm down. Probably just a deer.* There were a ton of deer in these woods. I mean, an actual *person* wouldn't be out this late, right? In this little patch of unknown woods behind a suburban neighborhood?

Right?

I glanced left. Upstream. Water rolling gently over the rocks, catching in the moonlight. I glanced right. The riverbank I climbed down, my shoes sitting on the stones—

Scrrrrp.

Every muscle in my body froze. Because that sound —that was undeniable. It wasn't a deer, or some woodland animal, or anything else.

It was the soft scuffing sound of a shoe on concrete.

Coming from right above me.

Someone's on the bridge. I held my breath, my entire body shaking. *Don't make a sound. Don't. Make. A. Sound.*

There was no way anyone would know I was down here. No way—

Except for my shoes on the rocks.

Scrrrrp.

Should I run? But the water was a foot deep, or more. Too slow. By the time I got to the riverbank, they'd already be there.

Stay here. Wait for them to pass. I slowly, carefully, sucked in a shuddering breath. *Probably just some drunk teenager, like Tina and I were. Or some high-as-fuck person stumbling their way home.* They probably didn't even notice the shoes.

Don't make a sound. I gripped the rough cement with my hands. Tried to stop my legs from shaking. Tried to stay as silent as I possibly could.

But it didn't matter.

Cling-bling!

My phone's text sound echoed off the concrete—and the limping footsteps immediately stopped.

No. No, no, no.

Dead silence rang in my ears. No crickets, no rustling of animals, no insects buzzing. Nothing. It was like whoever was up there... their presence had scared everything away.

Scrrrrp.

The footsteps resumed.

But this time, they were going the *other* direction.

Towards the riverbank.

Fear pounded through me. I lunged for my purse. "Come on, come on," I whispered as I rummaged through old lip balms and broken pens. I finally pulled out my phone, unlocked it, and began to dial 911—

Splash.

Oh fuck oh fuck they're in the water—

"911, what is your emergency?"

"I'm under the bridge behind—"

And then it happened.

I lost my balance on the concrete ledge. I scrambled for purchase, but I was already falling. The phone went flying out of my hands and plunked into the creek.

I fell face-down in the water.

Sound cut off. The cold water shocked my body like a thousand tiny needles pricking my skin. My hair fanned around me, tangling over my face.

Phone's gone.

No one knows you're here.

Run. Run as fast as you can.

I pushed myself up, sputtering.

A figure stood at the other end of the bridge.

Tall and thin, silhouetted by moonlight. Watching me. I couldn't see its face, yet somehow—its shape, the way it stood...

"T—Tina?"

She didn't move.

My arms shook underneath me as I pushed myself to stand. Stars swam in my vision. I leaned against the concrete ledge, feeling like every ounce of blood had drained from my body.

There's no way that's Tina.

Tina is fucking dead.

Get out—get out of there now.

My mind was screaming. But I couldn't force myself to move. It was like I was hypnotized, like I wanted so badly for it to be real that my body was frozen. "Tina," I whispered, the sound echoing off the concrete in ethereal hisses. "Tina, is that you?"

She slowly tilted her head.

And then she began walking towards me.

Splash. One step. *Splash.* Another. My heart pounded in my chest as she closed the gap between us, her face still hidden in shadow.

She stopped two feet away from me.

This close, I could almost make out the contours of her face. Her green eyes. Her curly hair. I could almost smell that vanilla-cinnamon-earthy smell, just like on the night we made our pact—

She raised her arms.

And then, in a split second, pushed me down.

My head plunged underwater. I opened my mouth to scream—and sucked in a mouthful of water. *Not Tina. It's not Tina.* Pain shot through my lungs. I pushed against the rocky floor, as hard as I could.

I broke the surface.

The tall, thin silhouette stood over me. Curly hair hung over her face. Teeth shined in the darkness as her lips pulled into a smile.

"It's your fault," she said in a low, gravelly voice.

I tried to scream—but all I could do was cough up the water I'd breathed in.

"It's your fault she's dead."

And then my head plunged back underwater.

Tina's sister. Her same tall, thin build. Her same curly

hair. No wonder I'd thought she was actually Tina, standing there at the other side of the bridge.

"She was on her way to you!" Tiffany's voice was muffled above the surface, but I could still hear her as I tried desperately to pull my head out of her grasp. "She was going to surprise you. Drive all night so you'd have the whole weekend together. But you didn't give a shit about her, did you? Didn't have even two minutes to text her back?"

I loved her.

"She had friends. She had me. But all she wanted was *you*."

My eyes blinked open underwater.

I reached out my arms up. Found Tiffany's wrist on my head. Dug my fingernails in as hard as I could.

She yelped in pain.

And then she let go.

I pushed myself up. Kicked off against the rocks. Ran as fast as I could through the water without looking back. I scrambled up the riverbank and broke into a sprint, coughing and lightheaded but pushing forward for one reason.

Tina.

It's been three years since Tina died.

Tiffany served a short sentence for assault and is living thousands of miles away on the west coast. I've moved to Dayton after graduating, working for the same company I had the internship with. I've started dating someone recently who seems really great.

Life has been good.

Except for the fact that Tina is still gone.

Every July 11th, around 11:30 PM, I make my way back home. I sneak into the woods and go down to the old creek. The path is overgrown now, but I still force my way down, even if it means fighting a few thorny bushes.

Then I sit under the old concrete bridge and listen to the murmurs of the stream.

Wondering if somehow, somewhere, Tina is listening with me.

MY PHONE IS TAKING STRANGE PHOTOS

I first noticed it a week ago. On Friday night, my boyfriend and I went out to dinner. When we got back to the car, I took a selfie of us.

It wasn't until later that night, while Ted was getting ready to leave my apartment, that I actually took a closer look at it. At first, I didn't see anything. Just Ted's and my face, filling most of the frame, with little space between us.

But in that little space...

"Hey, Ted?"

"Yeah?"

"What's that in the backseat?"

It looked like a white speck, in the darkness of the backseat. As if the flash were glinting off of something shiny. But the backseat was empty—at least I'd thought so. We'd gone in Ted's car, which he keeps clean, to an obsessive degree.

"Huh. Dunno," he replied, handing the phone back to me. "Maybe a bug?"

"I guess, it could be."

At the time, I didn't give it any more thought. There must have been something back there, like a soda can or a sweatshirt with a zipper, that was reflecting the light. No big deal.

But then it happened again.

The next night, I'd taken a picture of my cat, Thistle, playing on the bed. And when I took a closer look at the photo... there was that bright speck, again.

Underneath the bed.

I glanced at Thistle, still on the bed. Then I glanced at the shadows underneath. Nothing looked out of place. Frowning, I got on my hands and knees and slowly lowered my face to the floor. Looked past the floral comforter, into the darkness.

Nothing.

I turned my phone's flashlight on and looked again.

Nothing.

I shrugged and sat back down in my armchair, mindlessly browsing Facebook. *Thump!*—Thistle started jumping again, attacking her mouse plushie in the cutest way. I quickly tapped over to the camera, ready to get an in-action shot—

I froze.

In the camera's live video feed, there was the speck.

I glanced over my phone, at the darkness under my bed. Nothing there. Glanced back at my phone. The speck. I rubbed my finger over the camera's lens. Still there. I moved my phone back and forth, slowly, then tilted and rotated it.

The speck stayed. In the exact same place, under the bed.

... *What?*

Some weird glitch? With the video processing or the lighting or something? I sat there, confused, staring at my phone.

Then I put it down. Turned on all the lights. Thoroughly checked every inch of space under the bed. But there was nothing there—only dust bunnies and cat hair and a few old bobby pins.

Must have been the bobby pins, I thought, as I turned off the light and went to sleep.

I woke with a start at 4:07 AM.

My heart was racing a mile a minute. My sheets were covered in cold sweat. I fumbled for the glass of water on my nightstand. Took a deep breath in, let it out.

I couldn't even remember what my nightmare was about. I just remembered the fear. The need to run, as fast and as far away as I possibly could.

I took a sip of water and reached for my phone.

And then—I don't know why I did it, but I did. I opened the camera. And then, hands shaking, I swept it across the room. From my shelves of history books, to my *Le Chat Noir* poster, to my closed closet door.

Nothing.

I let out the breath I'd been holding. *Nothing's there. You're fine. Totally, completely fine.* I took in a deep breath, then slowly let it *whoosh* back out. *Nothing's there. You're safe.* I reached my thumb out on the screen, to tap back home.

But I missed.

My thumb hit the front-facing camera button.

No no no—

On the phone's screen, just over my shoulder. The glowing speck. Not a speck—an *eye*. Attached to the twisted, sunken face of a woman. Stringy black hair cascaded down her shoulders as she stared at me with one white, glowing eye. The other an empty, dark socket.

The phone fell from my hands. I turned around, screaming.

But there was only empty air behind me.

WOCKET IN MY POCKET

My son's favorite book is *There's a Wocket in My Pocket* by Dr. Seuss. So when I found a sequel on eBay, I was ecstatic.

It arrived three days after I ordered it. *There's a Zidge in your Fridge,* it said in big, bold letters across the cover. Showing a boy drawn in Dr. Seuss's signature style, opening the fridge and staring at a grumpy, pink-furred creature sitting atop of a carton of eggs.

"Do you ever see the ZIDGE in your FRIDGE?" I read in a silly voice as I sat on Jeremy's bed. He giggled.

I flipped to the first page. "Or the NOY LOX in your TOY BOX?" A green creature with spikes on its back, like a stegosaurus, held a little ball as the boy in the drawing held a baseball bat.

"Is there a noy lox in MY toy box?" Jeremy asked, grinning.

"We can pretend there is!"

I walked over to the toy box and flipped the lid open

and closed a few times. "Let's play baseball!" I said in a gruff little voice. Jeremy giggled. My bedtime stories were often full productions, with voice acting and props, and tonight was no different.

I sat back in bed, grinning.

But my smile faded when I flipped the page.

Do you ever see the LURTAN behind the CURTAIN? it read. The drawing showed a sparsely-decorated family room, with a large picture window flanked by deep purple curtains.

Sticking out from underneath the curtains were two feet.

They looked sort of like bird feet. Yellow talons with white claws. But the bump in the curtains was clearly not the shape of a bird.

"Why is it hiding?" Jeremy asked.

"I don't—"

I glanced up, at our own window, our own curtains. *I could've sworn...* I shook my head. *Of course they're moving. The AC's on full blast.*

I turned the page.

"When you dash by the TRASH, do you smell the BLASH?" I breathed a sigh of relief. This one was funny, again. A mustached monster with yellow-and-green fur poked out of the garbage can, almost looking like Oscar the Grouch. Poking out of his mouth was a half-eaten cheeseburger.

Jeremy laughed. I turned the page.

And stopped.

And in the MIRROR, when you get nearer, do you ever see the XIRROR?

The drawing showed the little boy looking in the mirror while brushing his teeth. Just behind him—poking out from behind his shoulder—was the "xirror."

But the xirror didn't look like a cute little creature.

It looked like the little boy.

I frowned and flipped past that page before Jeremy could protest. But it wasn't much better. "When you hear a noise, in your CLOSET, have you ever thought it was the YOSET?" The drawing showed the boy pulling open the double doors of his closet. Lying across the top shelf, among storage boxes and old shoes, was a tall, furry creature with glowing yellow eyes.

I began to turn the page—

Thump.

A soft sound, coming from the closet. So soft I could barely hear it over the rush of the AC.

I swallowed, my hands still on the page. Then I dropped the book on the bed and stood up, my heart pounding in my chest.

"Daddy? You didn't finish the story."

"I will in a second," I said, not taking my eyes off our own bifold closet doors. They were shut tight, the fake brass knobs glimmering in the glow of Jeremy's night light. The horizontal slats running up and down each door were dark. No yellow glowing eyes.

Oh, you think there's a monster in the closet, now?

Meredith is going to laugh her ass off when she gets back. You! Six-foot-three, a black belt in karate, scared of a kids' book!

The knot in my chest didn't loosen. I could see my

reflection in the doorknobs, now—and my terrified expression.

Calm down. There's nothing there.

But my hands shook as I reached out and grabbed the doorknobs. I sucked in a breath, and then with all of my strength, pulled them open—

The closet was empty.

Jeremy's clothes hung still and silent. Piles of junk, too-small socks and forgotten books, scattered the floor. I breathed out a sigh of relief. *Everything is fine. Everything is fine.*

I pulled the closet doors closed—

No.

Sticking out of the slats was a tuft of dark fur.

Snap. I yanked the closet doors back open. But there was nothing there. The top shelf was empty. Only boxes of scarves and coats, piles of old stuffed animals—

Stuffed animals. Right there by the edge, there was a stuffed gorilla, with black plasticky fur. *That must've been it.* I slowly closed the doors. They squeaked against the track.

"Daddy? Is everything okay?"

"Everything is fine," I said, walking back towards him. "I just thought I heard a sound, so I went to make sure there weren't any monsters in the closet."

"Like the yoset?"

"Yes, like the yoset."

"Are you going to finish the story?"

I sighed. "Yeah, I will."

I reached over and picked the book back up.

Glancing back at Jeremy, I sneakily skipped over the middle, and opened it to the last page.

"'Goodnight,' your Daddy said, and tucked you into BED. But, now I wonder—does *he* know about the VED?"

The drawing showed the little boy, sleeping in his bed. For a second, I didn't notice any creature—until I looked under the bed.

In the inky shadow there were two glowing, red eyes.

"Okay. That's the end," I said, putting the book on his nightstand and making a mental note to throw it out first thing tomorrow.

Surprisingly, Jeremy did not fight me on this. "Goodnight, Daddy."

"Goodnight, Jer."

I shut the door and walked out of the room, my legs still shaky. Then I walked over to the master bathroom and splashed cold water on my face.

Look at you. Still afraid of monsters and the dark.

You haven't changed one bit.

I reached for the towel and blotted my face dry. Sighing, I put it back on the rack.

And froze.

There was something standing behind me. No—some*one*. As soon as I looked at it, it disappeared. But I saw enough to know.

It looked exactly like me.

I ran out of the bathroom, my feet slipping against the floor. "Jeremy!" I shouted, as I burst into his room. "Jere—"

"Daddy."

He was sitting on the bed. Crying his eyes out. I ran over to him and wrapped my arms around him, holding him close. "You're okay. You're okay," I whispered.

He looked up at me, his eyes filled with tears.

"Daddy... I think there's something under my bed."

MY WIFE HATES HALLOWEEN

Phoebe has always hated Halloween.

Even back when we were dating—she never came to any Halloween parties with me. *I have a cold. I have a headache. I ate something bad.* After we got married and moved into the suburbs, she wouldn't even join me handing out candy to trick-or-treaters. *I'm going to sleep,* she'd say, even though it was only 6 o'clock. She'd even ask me to leave the house because I was "making too much noise."

I let it slide... until Anthony was born.

"Come on. We *have* to go trick-or-treating." Anthony was dressed up as the cutest little pumpkin— only 8 months old. He smiled as I bounced him in my arms, looking out the door into the night.

"I'm really not feeling well," Phoebe replied, lingering on the stairs.

"You seemed fine ten minutes ago."

"Well, I don't feel well *now*."

"I don't believe you." It was mean, but I was annoyed. She'd given me the same excuses for eight Halloweens in a row. It wasn't coincidence.

She didn't deny it—just looked past me, into the night.

"Why do you hate Halloween? Is it because your parents were so strict? I know you weren't allowed to trick-or-treat, growing up..."

"Can't you just take Anthony alone?"

"I want to go as a family."

She glanced again at the darkness gathering outside. Then she pressed her lips into a thin line. "I'm sorry. But I don't feel good."

A heavy silence settled between us.

She came down the stairs. Wrapped her arms around both of us, and patted Anthony softly on the head. "I love you both. Have fun tonight."

From the way her voice slightly wavered, I could've sworn she was on the verge of tears. But she turned away, and in a flash of dark hair, she was already upstairs.

The same dance happened over and over again, every year. Anthony was soon wearing Mutant Ninja Turtles and Star Wars costumes instead of pumpkins, but Phoebe still refused to go trick-or-treating with us. Every year we had the same discussion. I asked her to come. She insisted that she was feeling ill. She went upstairs to our bedroom and locked the door. Anthony and I headed out onto the sidewalk, candy bucket swinging.

Except, on the evening of Halloween 2021, we came home early.

Anthony had tripped and skinned his knee. So less than an hour after we left we were hobbling home. As we rounded the bend onto Maple Ave., I saw that the light in our room was on.

Phoebe hadn't "gone to sleep" like she said she was.

I helped Anthony with the wound, set him up in front of the TV, and then charged upstairs. I was mad. She must've heard us come home, must've heard Anthony crying in the kitchen—and she didn't even come down to check on us? Whether her aversion to Halloween was psychological, or some sort of moral religious thing, it had to stop.

But as I got to the top of the stairs, I froze.

Phoebe's voice was coming from our room.

She was talking to someone.

I tiptoed to the door and pressed my ear against it. I couldn't make out what she was saying—but her voice was low, fast, soft. Like she was trying not to be heard.

My body went cold. I turned the doorknob—but it was locked.

"Phoebe! Let me in!"

The light coming from under the door went out.

"I know you're in there," I shouted.

Seconds ticked by. A clatter sounded from behind the door. Then, finally, it opened.

Phoebe darted out, quickly closing the door behind her. She looked significantly worse than just an hour ago, her skin was pale and deep bags under her eyes. "You shouldn't be home this early," she whispered.

"Who's in there with you?"

"No one." She glanced back at the closed door. "You and Anthony need to get out of here. *Now.*"

"What's going on?"

"Mike—"

She was cut off by a soft *thump*.

Someone was knocking on our bedroom door.

Something about the knocks made my whole body go cold. They were slow, methodical—like the person on the other side had all the time in the world.

"Who's in there?" I whispered.

She glanced back at the door again, her eyes wide. "Do you remember the time I got a really bad asthma attack? I told you about it when we first started dating. How I was in the hospital for weeks, how I almost died."

Thump... thump...

"What's that got to do with anything?"

"I should've died. But I didn't. And now—every Halloween—I have to give *it* some of my life, in payment."

Without another word, she pushed the door open.

In the center of the darkened room stood a towering form. Black robes hung off its thin frame, trailing on the ground. A large jack-o'-lantern sat on its shoulders, its eyes flickering amber, the mouth cut into a wide grin. The only parts of its body visible were its hands—long, gray, bone-thin fingers that ended in sharp nails.

It stood in the center of the room, absolutely still.

Phoebe turned away from me. She walked towards the thing, her legs shaking underneath her. The jack-o'-lantern raised a bony finger and touched her forehead.

And then it crumpled into a mass of black fabric at her feet.

Phoebe turned around. Her mouth stretched into a wide grin as her eyes locked on mine. Then she stepped toward me, emitting a horrible, guttural laugh.

I ran out of the bedroom.

"Anthony!" I shouted. Finding him still in front of the TV, I grabbed him and ran outside. We leapt into the car and peeled out of the driveway. In the rearview mirror, I could see her—its—silhouette in the upstairs window.

Watching us.

THE VENDING MACHINE

There's a vending machine on campus that doesn't just dispense snacks.

It sits in the basement of Fowler Hall, even though the laundry machines were moved upstairs years ago. All the other ones have been updated into sleek, futuristic models—but not this one. It looks like it was plucked right out of the '90s, with its smudged glass display and silver coils holding snacks. Its red sign glows brightly in the darkness, through the musty haze, simply reading: **REFRESHMENTS.**

To be honest, I didn't really believe the urban legends surrounding the thing. But I work for the campus newspaper, and for Halloween, I got assigned to write this stupid fluff piece about it.

The most popular legend about it goes like this: on a dark and stormy night, a sociology major went down into the basement of Fowler, craving an ice-cold bottle of coke. But when he got it out of the machine, he realized it wasn't filled with the sugary delight he so craved—but a murky, red-brown sludge!

The story diverges from there. Some say he drank it and died. Others say he turned it into the police, and it matched the remains of a local missing woman. Still others say the bottle cursed him, and he went on an all-out murder spree that miraculously wasn't covered by a single news outlet...

Yeah. You see where I'm going with this.

There are other stories that follow a similar theme. A junior pressed the button for pretzels and got a human finger. Or she got a cursed knife, and cut off somebody's finger. Or her own finger got cut off when she pushed the flap to retrieve her drink. It depends on who you asked—everyone tells a different version. There are even a few stories that diverge from the whole murdery thing. Some CS majors told me if you pressed a certain code into the keypad, the vending machine would slide away and reveal a secret room. Of course, none of them could decide on what the code actually was...

Yeah. I didn't believe any of this shit for a second.

My final bit of research, though, was to actually go down there and use it myself. So there I was, standing outside of Fowler Hall a little past ten PM, coins jingling in my pockets.

"So what do you think you'll get?" Breanna asked me.

She worked on the newspaper with me—and believed all the stories. Apparently one of her sorority sisters knew the girl who got the finger. Or lost her finger. Or whatever. "I think I'll get a nice, refreshing root beer," I replied with a smile. Then I cupped my hand over my mouth. "Oh, I shouldn't say that. It can hear us, right?"

Breanna rolled her eyes. "Come on. That stuff really did happen. Yeah, some people exaggerated it and it kinda snowballed into an urban legend, but that girl really did lose her finger."

Honestly, of all the stories I'd heard, that was the only one that sounded like it could be true. Sticking your hand in a thirty-year-old machine that's all rusted up and half-broken... I don't think she lost her finger, but she probably got a bad cut and had to get a tetanus booster or something.

But then we rounded the corner.

And I couldn't help the chill that tingled down my spine.

It didn't match the other students' descriptions at all. It wasn't all rusted and dented and broken, with 20-year-old potato chips in it. Far from it. In fact, it seemed like the only thing that was cleaned regularly in this entire basement. The **REFRESHMENTS** lettering glowed brightly; the snacks and drinks were perfectly nestled in their steel coils, not one of them askew. The boxes and chairs surrounding it were covered in a thick film of dust, but the vending machine sparkled.

Even though this basement was an abandoned storage area, someone had been cleaning the machine —regularly.

I stepped right up to the glass. On the other side was a perfectly normal assortment of drinks and snacks:

potato chips, Oreos, Cheetos, chocolate bars, and a line of sodas on the bottom. As my eyes hit the root beer, my stomach did a little flip.

I drank that brand of root beer. So I was all too familiar with the advertisement on the wrapper, the one with the stylized Dracula, offering a chance to win free Six Flags tickets.

That was from Halloween, this year.

Someone had restocked this machine. Recently.

"Who's restocking this thing?" I whispered, leaning so close to the glass that I could see my own reflection. "I thought nobody came down here."

"Maybe the janitor?"

I glanced at the clumps of dust sticking to the feet of the machine, the row of folding chairs leaning askew. "I don't think they really come down here."

"Well, are you going to get something?" Breanna cocked an eyebrow at me. "Or are you *scared?*"

"Of course I'm not scared."

I reached into my pocket and pulled out seven quarters. $1.75. Then I plunked each one into the coin slot. *Clink, clang, clack.* I listened to each one clink deep inside the machine.

Then I slowly lifted my finger up to the keypad and pressed **F6**.

The machine rumbled softly. My eyes shot to the coil, slowly unwinding to let the root beer fall. I watched that stupid stylized Dracula face as the bottle teetered on the edge—and then plunged into the bin below.

Thump.

I stood, frozen. Staring at the little black flap. At the four letters engraved in the plastic, P U S H.

"What are you waiting for?"

"I'm thinking," I snapped back.

"You're scared." She let out a giggle.

"No. I'm not. I'm just..." I shook my head. "Whatever."

I crouched down, until the flap was nearly at eye level. Then I reached out—and pushed my hand through the flap.

The metal interior was cold against my skin. I felt around, reaching for the bottle. *Huh. Where is it?* My heart beat faster as my fingers stretched out against all the sides. I didn't believe those legends, but I also didn't like blindly groping around in this little metal box. What if there was like, a dead mouse in there? Or something sharp?

I reached in further—

And froze.

Something touched me. Oh, God, something touched me. I yanked my hand out, the PUSH flap swinging in the darkness, backing away from the machine—

"There a problem?"

"S-something touched me."

"Oh, so now you believe the stories, huh?"

"I—"

"I'll get it for you." Before I could stop her, Breanna crouched down. Stuck her hand in. Rooted around. "Ah, found it. Right th—"

She let out a howl.

"Breanna!" I screamed, rushing over.

She tried to pull her hand out. Tried to back away. "It's—it's stuck," she cried. "Help me."

I wrapped my arms around her waist and tried to pull her back. But she was right—something was holding her in place. Or—*oh, God*—some*one*? I dug my heels into the carpet, pulling with all my strength. But she didn't budge. I glanced at her arm—the flap was nearly at her elbow now, like something was *pulling her in*—

And then I heard laughter.

The blood drained out of my face. The shadows shifted in the murky hallway, and then two of my classmates stepped out from behind the vending machine.

"The look on your face," Tori wheezed through giggles.

"I can't believe you fell for that," Allison added.

I opened my mouth. But no words came out. I worked my jaw, glancing at each of their faces. Even Breanna was in hysterics now.

"Why... why would you do that?" I asked, finally, in a weak voice.

"Oh, come on, it's just a prank," Breanna said. "And now you've got something to write about."

"You're not mad, are you?" Allison asked, with fake concern.

Hot tears were welling in my eyes. But I blinked them away. *How could I be so stupid?* A cursed vending machine, really? All the people who told me those stories... they must've been in on it, too. I should've known joining the newspaper was a bad idea. Half the team were mean-girl types, in Phi Gamma whatever. Of course they would do something like this.

Bitches.

"Of course I'm not mad," I said, plastering on a fake smile. "That was really funny. You totally had me."

Disappointment flickered across Breanna's face. Then she quickly recovered. "Well, we need to get going if we're going to make it to Charles's party," she said. "You coming with?"

I shook my head.

I watched as the three of them—tall, blonde, almost comically Barbie-like—walked back down the hallway and disappeared around the corner.

Then it was just me and the vending machine.

I poked my head around the back. The lock on the back door was rusted and mangled; probably didn't even work. The cavity where the drinks would fall out opened up back here, too—which is how one of them leaned in to grab Breanna's hand. The root beer I'd paid for sat forgotten on the ground.

I leaned over and picked it up.

I walked back into the hallway and sat down on the floor. Twisted the cap off, listened to the hiss of air escaping. The red glow of the **REFRESHMENTS** sign spilled out onto the dusty carpet.

Tears fell from my cheeks as I lifted the bottle to my lips.

But as soon as the root beer hit my tongue, I realized something was wrong.

A soft *thump* sounded from the machine. Too soft,

too metallic, to be a bottle of soda or a bag of chips. I slowly got up, walked over to it.

The rows of chips and sodas stood perfectly still. Untouched. I crouched down, in front of the flap, my fingers hesitating in mid-air. I glanced up at the sign, the red light spilling onto my face, onto my tears.

I pushed my hand inside.

Unlike the first time, I found it immediately.

It was a small envelope. Nothing written on either side. I flipped it over in my hands—then opened it and slipped out its contents.

Three photographs.

I recognized the faces immediately. Breanna. Tori. Allison. But each photo showed them in a compromising position. Breanna making out with a guy who wasn't her boyfriend. Tori smoking something out of a bong. Allison... well, before plastic surgery made her into the Allison I knew.

I looked up at the machine and smiled.

Apparently, the rumors are true—

There is something very, *very* special about the vending machine in the basement of Fowler Hall.

MY SON WENT MISSING

My 6-year-old son wandered off into the woods behind our house.

I thought he was in his room, playing with Legos. But when I checked on him twenty minutes later, he was gone.

After tearing apart the house looking for him, I noticed the back door was unlocked. *No. He ran out and... someone took him.*

I went catatonic. I called the police, my husband came home, and an all-out search began. When we looked at our security cam footage, it showed little Parker simply walking across the backyard... and wandering into the forest.

"Okay," I breathed. "So he's just lost. As long as we find him soon, everything will be okay."

And it was the happiest moment of my life when, three hours later–right after dusk–one of our neighbors in the search party found him.

"Parker," I sobbed as I held him. So happy that he'd come home safe.

But that evening, my happiness started to fade.

You see, my son Parker is neurodivergent. He's high-functioning, but he still has a lot of quirks that aren't normal for a kid his age. He's obsessed with birds—he can identify everything from the northern mockingbird to the downy woodpecker, and would rather do that than hang out with other kids any day. Food textures bother him to no end, especially dairy, and even just watching me drink a cup of milk or eat yogurt makes him retch in disgust. He throws a fit if anything gets wet—even a drop of water on the tablecloth will send him spiraling.

So imagine my surprise when I spilled a glass of water at the dinner table—and Parker didn't react at all.

Normally he'd be grabbing the tablecloth and running over to the dryer, screaming at me to get it dry. But instead he just sat there, oddly still, eating his chicken nuggets.

I guess he's just too wiped out to care.

But as I mopped up the water, I couldn't shake that horrible feeling in the pit of my stomach.

Later that evening, I sat next to Parker's racecar bed, perusing the bookshelf for a book. It was a hard choice—a favorite, like *There's a Wocket in Your Pocket?* Or should I make him up one of my silly tales about Iris the Ibis?

I felt like this night wasn't real. Like I was dreaming that Parker was here, safely tucked into bed, and that soon I was going to wake up to him being still missing, still gone. I swallowed that thought and focused on my beautiful boy's face, fighting back the tears welling in my eyes.

"Do you want Dr. Seuss, or a story about Iris?" I asked him.

He tilted his head. "Dr. Seuss," he said after a second.

"Okay." I opened the book and began to read. He didn't notice the tears rolling down my cheeks.

Soon it was over and I was turning out the lights. But as I turned on my heel, he called after me. "Can I have milk?"

I stopped in the doorway.

"Uh... sure," I said, my heart pounding in my ears.

Something woke me in the middle of the night.

3:26 AM, read the time on my phone. *Still 3 hours before I have to be up.* I sighed, pulled the covers around me, and rolled over—

I froze.

The door was open.

And there, peeking around the corner—

Was Parker.

He was just standing there. Watching me sleep. Watching *us* sleep. And maybe it was my imagination... but in the darkness, it looked like he was smiling.

"Parker?"

He dipped out of view and began to run down the hallway. "Parker—wait!" I called out, jumping out of bed. "Parker!"

I ran out of the room just in time to see him disappear into his bedroom. But I couldn't breathe. Couldn't move.

Because he'd been running down the hallway...

On all fours.

I woke up before Parker did. Unable to shake the jittery feeling in my stomach, I busied myself by mixing up some from-scratch pancake batter and dusting off our waffle maker. *Parker's safe. This calls for a special breakfast,* I told myself.

Then why did I feel like something was so horribly wrong?

I poured the thick batter into the waffle maker. It sizzled on contact. As I closed the lid, though, my phone began to ring.

FRANKLIN POLICE, read the caller ID. *Huh.* "Hello?"

"Mrs. Zimmerman?" a deep voice asked.

"Yeah?"

"This is the Franklin Police Department," the voice replied. "And I'm thrilled to tell you: we found your son."

Every muscle in my body froze. "... What?"

"Someone apparently found him in the development on the other side of the woods, only an hour after he went missing. They've been trying to get in contact with us, but we only just got a hold of them now. He's here at the police station. Would you like to talk to him?"

I opened my mouth, but no sound came out. The phone was slippery in my sweat-covered hands. "I—I don't understand," I said finally. "We... a neighbor... found Parker... last night. But—but you're saying... Parker's with you at the station?"

Before he could reply, I heard a soft footstep behind me.

I whipped around to find Parker was standing in the doorway of the kitchen, his ice-blue eyes fixed on me.

"Mommy," he said softly, "who's on the phone?"

MY MOM'S GARDEN

When my stepdad passed away, I moved back in with my mom.

Initially, she wasn't doing so well. But after a couple weeks, she took up a new hobby that seemed to change her outlook on life: gardening. I know, I should've been happy. I mean, it was better than locking herself in her bedroom crying all day, right?

But...

It was weird. Gardening is the *last* thing I would expect my mom to do. She's a very fast-paced, independent businesswoman type. She doesn't cook, she isn't crafty, and she absolutely hates the outdoors. The bugs, the sunburns, the pollen allergies—all of it.

"And she's so weird about it," I told my boyfriend over the phone. "Like a few days ago, she found me in the garden, and she *flipped out*. And did I tell you she only works on it at night? She says it's because she sunburns. But you have to admit, it's super weird."

"Okay, yes, it's a little odd. But that's probably when she's feeling the most lonely," Matt offered.

I paced into the kitchen. Even though it was almost midnight, I could see her dim silhouette just beyond the back porch light. Hunched over the garden bed.

"She's out there *right now*," I whispered, even though she couldn't possibly hear. "I'm worried about her."

"I know you are, Ali. But it's only been a few months—"

"Richard wasn't even that great! He was constantly spending her money. He didn't have a job, but he was always getting the latest iPhone, Airpods, laptops..."

"Ali," he warned.

"At least they were only married five years. Imagine if he lived longer. She wouldn't have anything left—"

"*ALI!*" Matt shouted into the phone.

I sucked in a shaky breath. "Okay, okay. Sorry. He wasn't *that* bad. I just... I dunno. It hurts that she's like a thousand times sadder about his death than Dad's."

"I get it. But you have to be nice. And support her. Okay?"

"Okay."

"Give her time. *Let her be.*"

"You're right."

But when I hung up the phone, I opened the door and walked right down to the garden. Maybe it was rude, but that's why I was here, as Matt said. To support her. To keep an eye on her. To help her get on her feet.

"Oh, hi, Alison," she said, straightening. "Shouldn't you be asleep?"

"Shouldn't you?"

"I guess so. But I just wanted to get a little more work done in the garden." She pulled her bare hands out of the soil, her fingernails caked with black dirt.

Gone were the days of perfect French gel manicures, I guess. "We should get you some gardening gloves."

"I like to feel the soil under my bare hands."

"What are you planting?" I asked, crouching next to her.

"Just some vegetables."

"Which ones?"

"Well... I've got some radishes over there," she said, pointing to the far end of the bed. "And I was thinking of putting some carrots over here."

"Aren't you allergic to carrots?"

"They'd be for you."

"Oh," I said lamely. "Thanks. That's really nice."

"Of course." She brushed a bit of dirt from her cheek with the back of her hand. "Now, why don't you head to bed? I don't want to keep you up, and I'll be in soon."

So she wanted to get rid of me.

I almost protested, but then I remembered Matt's words. *Let her be.* I forced a smile and stood up. "Okay. Goodnight, Mom."

"Goodnight, hun."

I realized it as I was falling asleep.

I'd been just drifting off, my thoughts stretching into strange and illogical dreams like pieces of taffy. And then four words popped in my head, screaming for attention:

She wasn't planting anything.

The entire time I was out there, talking to her. She was just... sticking her fingers into the dirt. Pulling them out. Scratching at the top of the soil, then patting it down. It was like that scene from Monty Python with the peasants. They look like they're doing work, but they're just stacking mud, over and over and over.

What if...

What if it wasn't a garden? What if it was just a four-by-eight rectangle of empty dirt, that she kept playing with, every day, for hours on end?

I rolled over, listening to my mom's footsteps in the adjacent room. Then the creak of the bed as she stepped up into it.

What if she just... snapped?

I stood up and walked over to the window. Outside I could see the garden, illuminated by the full moon. The large rectangular bed of freshly-turned dirt, the fence surrounding it.

Memories flashed through my mind of the hours I'd seen my mom, hunched over the garden bed. Digging and pulling at the dirt with her bare hands, her fingernails caked with it, the darkness seeping into every wrinkle. Her eyes focused downwards, never looking up.

I've never seen her plant a seed. Never watched her dig a hole and put a plant in.

I'd only seen her bent over, pushing, pulling, tearing, raking her fingers through the earth.

Oh, Mom...

I had to know. I *had* to. I stood frozen in front of the window for fifteen minutes or so, waiting until I was sure she was asleep. Then I crept down the stairs and walked into the backyard.

The summer air was alive. Crickets chirping, frogs croaking, a few lightning bugs dancing in the darkness. I turned on my phone's flashlight and walked to the back of our yard, where the garden sat. I unlocked the gate and stepped inside. A narrow gravel path surrounded the raised bed in the center: a four-by-eight cedar construction, filled to the brim with garden soil.

I started at the corner where she said she planted radishes.

I stuck my fingers into the damp earth. Scraped away at the layers of soil. Pawed and sifted and examined.

There was nothing.

No seeds, no seedlings, nothing. Just dirt and dirt and more dirt. "No," I whispered, backing away from the bed.

And then I saw it.

Something glinting in the dirt.

I stood up. Slowly walked over to it, crouched down. Yes—there it was—something shiny poking out of the soil. I leaned over, brushed the dirt away with my thumb. *Glass?* Oh, no, Mom. You could've cut your fingers up on this.

I grabbed the glass—and pulled.

Out of the dirt came a pair of glasses.

A familiar pair. Wire-frames. Thick square lenses.

Grief shot through my heart as I stared at them, and my hands trembled.

They were my stepdad's.

My thought was a crazy one, but I wasn't going to risk it.

My car crawled up the steep hill to Fairview Cemetery. Pink light bled through the clouds on the horizon, and a flock of birds dotted the sky. I yawned. I hadn't gotten a wink of sleep—I'd just lay there, confused and terrified, waiting until dawn.

The air was still as I parked my car. Dew clung to the grass and wet my boots as I walked through the tombstones. I fidgeted with the pair of glasses in my pocket, chewing my lip. And then I was there—standing in front of Richard's tombstone.

I let out a sigh of relief.

The dirt was perfectly intact. Sprigs of grass popped up through the dark dirt, and a bouquet of wilted flowers lay on top.

Did I really think she...?

I mean, the four-by-eight bed was a perfect size to bury someone. Especially someone tall, like Richard. And I could've sworn he'd been buried in *those* glasses...

I shook my head.

She didn't. It was fine. Everything was fine.

I walked back to the car, the pink glow deepening into orange that glowed as brightly as smelted steel. I opened the door, took a breath of the fresh spring air, and began the drive home. I'd ask Mom about the garden later, but for now, I was at least reassured she wasn't a total psychopath.

But when I opened the front door, the house was empty.

"Mom?" I called, as I walked into the kitchen. The bitter smell of coffee hung in the air, which meant she had to be around here somewhere. "Mom!" I shouted, my voice echoing against the walls.

Nothing.

A cup of half-drunk coffee sat on the table. Next to a muffin, untouched. The sense of unease in my stomach grew. "Mom? Where are you?"

The glass door slid open behind me.

I jumped a foot in the air. "Oh my gosh, Mom. You scared me. You're out there so early? I thought the sun—"

"You were in my garden last night. Weren't you?"

My mom's blue eyes bore into mine. They were cold, examining—none of her usual warmth. I swallowed. "Um, yeah, about that—"

"*What did you do?*"

I froze. She sounded so accusatory, so panicked. "Nothing! I didn't do anything! But you..." I trailed off, trying to figure out how to word it gently. "You're not planting anything. It's just empty dirt. And I, I found Richard's glasses out there. What... what are you doing, Mom?"

She shook her head frantically. "No. *No.* You messed up everything. Where are his glasses, Alison? *Where?!*"

"Mom—"

"*Where are his glasses?!*"

My hands were shaking. I'd never seen Mom this mad—not even when I flunked Algebra in tenth grade.

"Th-they're right here," I said, reaching into my pocket.

She snatched them out of my hands.

Then, without another word, she stormed out of the room.

I watched as she sprinted across the backyard. Fumbled with the garden door. Hunched over the bed and pawed at the dirt like a wild animal. I could see her lips moving, as if she were muttering something to herself, over and over.

I collapsed into one of the kitchen chairs and began to sob.

"She won't go to a therapist?"

"No."

I was at wit's end. After our big fight, she'd eventually calmed down. She even apologized a bunch of times for her outburst. But... when I suggested going to a therapist, or at least a grief counselor, she vehemently refused. *I can't, I can't,* she kept saying, over and over.

"I want to help her. But I don't know how anymore." I sucked in a breath through sobs. "Clearly she's... she's not getting better."

"I'm sorry. I don't know what to tell you," Matt replied.

The next few days, things got worse. Mom spent more time on the garden than ever, hauling huge bags of soil amendments inside—bone meal, blood meal, compost. I watched as she worked it all into the soil, her fingers furiously digging into the earth.

But no plants grew.

Not even weeds.

I felt powerless. Like my mom was spiraling into madness and I couldn't do anything to help. I tried to take her out, buy her things, spend time with her. But she spent more and more time in the garden, less and less with me.

"I could call the police and ask for a wellness check on her."

"I don't know if that's a good idea."

"She's getting worse, Matt."

I didn't want to turn to extreme measures. Calling the police would mean breaking her trust forever. But maybe that was better than... this.

It was getting ridiculous. I'd find dirty handprints on the refrigerator door. Little trails of black dirt meandering from the back door to Richard's old rocking chair to Mom's bedroom. Mom wasn't just relegating her garden work to nighttime now, either, and her fair skin was sunburned quite badly.

About a week later, I couldn't take it anymore.

I decided to do something drastic.

I waited until I heard the familiar *creak* of the mattress. Then I waited about an hour after that, straining my ears for any sound, making sure she was asleep for the night. When I was sure, I tiptoed down the hallway, crept over to the back door, and turned the lock.

I pulled the door open and stepped into the damp grass.

The night was dark. A crescent moon hung above me in the black sky. No crickets chirping, no frogs croaking—just the soft rustle of branches in the wind. I turned back to look at the house, one last time. My mom's window was still dark.

Good.

I swung the garden gate open. It creaked softly on its hinges. Then I stepped onto the pathway and stared down at the garden bed. No plants, no weeds, just dirt that was pitch black in the waning moonlight.

I grabbed the shovel, leaned up against the garden fence.

And then I plunged it into the dirt.

I pulled a shovelful out, my arms aching with the weight. Dumped it onto the ground. Then another. And another—

My shovel hit something.

My heart dropped. Slowly, carefully, I crouched down to the garden bed.

Something pale was poking through the dark earth.

With shaking hands, I reached down and brushed away the dirt. First slowly—then frantically. My lungs burned as I held my breath. *What the hell is—*

No.

I was staring at my own face.

Skin whitish pale—the color of roots that never saw the sun. Eyelids fused shut—but translucent enough that I could see the dark irises underneath. Thin, hair-like protrusions grew out of the pores, like little roots sapping up all that the soil had to offer.

I stepped back. *No. No...*

Crunch.

I whipped around.

Mom was standing behind me.

But there was someone next to her. A silhouette that moved strangely, as if it didn't yet know how to walk. But I recognized the build. The wire-frame glasses, as he stepped towards me...

Richard.

Richard, dirt caked in the corners of his eyes, underneath his fingernails. The same root-like protrusions growing all over his skin. His eyes fixed at me, the pupils jittering slightly. Then his mouth stretched into a crooked smile, revealing teeth caked with dirt.

Mom wrapped her arms around him and smiled. "You were never going to accept Richard," she said softly, into the silent night.

"Mom..." I cried out.

"We wanted to be a happy family," she said, her blue eyes locked on mine. "But you were standing in our way. But then... I got this idea... well, Richard got the idea. And now we'll be a happy family. Forever. Right, Richard?"

He stepped towards me, his grin widening. The smell of wet, rotting leaves filled my nose. He bent down, with jerky movements, and reached for the shovel at my feet.

I glanced at the garden fence. Six feet of steel. Mom

was standing against the gate, smiling as she watched Richard raise the shovel.

"No—Mom, please—"

"I love you, Allison."

The shovel came down with a dull *thump*.

And then everything went black.

ARE YOU DREAMING RIGHT NOW?

I saw the first one yesterday.

I was at the library with my kids. As they picked out their books I meandered around, bored, until something caught my eye. Next to one of those "reading is fun!" encouragement signs, there was a poster, reading in big letters:

ARE YOU DREAMING RIGHT NOW?

Intrigued, I stepped closer. There were instructions underneath, with cute minimalistic drawings next to each step.

1. *Look at the time on your phone, watch, or other device.*
2. *Look away for a few seconds.*
3. *Look back at the time.*

If the time doesn't match, you may be dreaming.

Remember, "pinching yourself" is just an old wives' tale. This is the only proven method. Remember to check early—and often!

I frowned. *What a weird sign.* I glanced around the library; no one seemed to be looking at it, or paying any attention to it at all. The old guy at the desk was glued to his laptop, the librarian was furiously sorting through the returned book bin, and my children were gabbing excitedly in the children's corner.

Just for kicks, I looked at the large clock hanging above the reception desk. The golden-metallic hands showed 12:08.

Then I looked at the floor. *1, 2, 3.*

Back at the clock. 12:08.

I found myself breathing a sigh of relief, even though I wasn't the slightest bit concerned that I was dreaming. Seriously, if this were a dream right now, there'd either be cat-faced dragons flying through the sky or a very naked Henry Cavill standing in front of me... or it would be that weird nightmare I keep having, about the man who crawls along the floor like a snake.

I turned away from the sign, to the New Releases shelf in front of me. I pulled out a thriller and paged through it for a while, until my kids were rocketing to the reception desk and nearly throwing their library cards at the poor librarian.

"Ava! Benjamin!" I barked, jogging to catch up with them.

"*Sorry!*"

By the time we got home, I'd forgotten all about the weird poster. I watched the kids play some video games, threw food in the Instant Pot, read more of the thriller. It was a good day.

But then I saw another poster.

The next day, while the kids were at school, I went grocery shopping. As I sped through the empty aisles, throwing bread and mayonnaise into the cart, I saw another poster.

It was stuck to the bulletin board near the checkout lanes. Next to an ad for a local math tutor, there was a smaller version of the exact same poster I'd seen at the library.

ARE YOU DREAMING RIGHT NOW?

"What's that sign about?" I asked the teenage girl ringing up my items.

She turned around to look at it. "Oh. Huh. That's kinda weird," she said with a chuckle. "I have no idea."

"It's kind of creepy, right?"

She shrugged. "Maybe that's the point? Like a prank to creep people out. It was just Halloween and all..."

On the ride home, I couldn't help but think about the sign. *Are you dreaming right now?* It was so stupid. Of all things, that shouldn't scare me. I'm a midwife—I deal with blood and pain and emergencies every day of the week.

I turned up the radio and focused on the kids' lunches. *Turkey for Ava... ham for Benjamin... I'll have to put the mayo on in the morning for Ava—she hates soggy bread. And Benjamin, I'll put a yogurt in for him, since he doesn't like cheese on his sandwich.*

Man, my kids are so picky.

My kids...

My stomach suddenly dropped.

What if the last ten years of my life have been a dream?

What if my kids... don't actually exist?

I couldn't help it. I glanced down at the car clock. 1:37 PM. I looked up at the road, focusing on the twisted trunk of an oak. *1, 2, 3...* Glanced down at the clock again.

1:37 PM.

I let out a breath I didn't realize I'd been holding. *Focus, Julia,* I told myself, sucking in a deep breath. *Breathe.* My life was not a dream. My kids definitely existed. Even by that stupid sign's standards, I wasn't dreaming. The clock read the same time.

Breathe... breathe...

I pulled into the driveway and stepped out of the car, my legs a little shaky. Went over to the trunk and hauled the groceries out of the back.

For the rest of the day, I pushed all my thoughts about that stupid poster out of my mind.

I woke up with a start.

My heart was pounding. Like I'd just woken up from a nightmare—although I couldn't remember having one.

I glanced at the bedside clock. 2:05 AM.

Not time to get up yet.

I rolled over and closed my eyes.

But something nagged at me. An unsettling feeling, growing in the pit of my stomach. I lifted my head and looked back over my shoulder at the bedside clock.

4:04 AM.

My heart dropped.

I'm dreaming.

Okay. So I'm dreaming. No reason to freak out. I glanced around the room—nothing was weird about this dream yet. No extra rooms, no upside-down furniture, no snakemen. No Henry Cavill either. Just me sitting alone on the bed—

Creeeeaaaak.

I whipped around.

The door to our bedroom was hanging open.

Dammit. It's this stupid fucking nightmare again.

My heart began to pound. Even though I knew it was a dream now, unlike every other time, it was hard to stop the fear. A lot of dreams are like that—you know? Just raw, powerful emotions. Even if the dream isn't that scary. Even if you know it's just a dream.

It's not real. I sucked in a breath. *Just. A. Dream.*

A soft rustling sound came from the darkness to my left. From the floor. I looked over the side of my bed to see a shape in the darkness. A shape I was all too familiar with. A man crawling along the floor, trying to be as quiet as possible.

This isn't real. None of this is real.

See? The clock says—

4:05.

The blood drained out of my face.

No. No, it can't be.

I looked down at the shadow on the floor. *1... 2... 3.* Looked back at the clock.

4:05.

No.

He was real. I must've fallen back asleep, after I looked at the clock the first time. It wasn't a dream. All this time, it wasn't a nightmare.

I opened my mouth and screamed.

WIND PHONE

I don't believe that anyone here on Earth can speak to the dead.

Or, at least—I didn't until yesterday.

But the concept was interesting. The original "wind phone" was an art installation in Japan, but now there are hundreds around the world. It's comprised of an empty phonebooth with an old rotary phone in it, usually placed in a garden or another peaceful place. You go there and pretend to call up one of your deceased loved ones.

Yesterday, I noticed that one had been installed in our town's botanical gardens.

It stood out starkly among the greenery. A white phone booth with glass-paneled sides. Probably made from one of the old phonebooths that used to line Main Street. I parked the car and walked towards it, the gravel crunching under my heels.

The inside was plain. A metal shelf holding a pad of

paper, a pen, and an old rotary phone made of shiny black plastic. There was a wooden chair, and as I sat down, it creaked loudly. Outside the windows, patches of bright purple zinnias bowed in the wind, and the pond rippled.

Should I do it?

Of all the people I've lost over the years, one stood front and center. Over and over again, in the middle of the night, he'd pop into my head. Sometimes I'd dream about him. It was like he haunted me. Almost ten years gone and he was still living in my head.

I picked up the phone.

"Hi, David. ...Um, I don't really know what to say. This is weird." I let out a forced laugh. "Okay. I guess I'll start by telling you everything that's happened... since you left."

That was a nice way of putting it. A mangled mess of metal and blood at the bottom of the mountain...

"I finally got that art degree. But in sculpture, not painting. Weird, right? But it's even more fun than painting. I just never got to do it in school."

Silence. Of course.

"And then last year, I got married. To William D_, of all people. We reconnected after college and settled back down here in town and... well..."

I trailed off. *Great idea, Sara, go ahead and tell David you married one of his high school friends. I bet he'd fucking love that.*

"Nevermind. Anyway. The Lakewood movie theater's a gym now. And you know that rock in Highpoint park, that overlooks the whole town? Where we'd sit for hours, watching the cars and the people on Main Street? It's all overgrown with brush now. I don't think I could get there if I tried. Maybe with a machete or something..."

My laugh echoed into the receiver. It sounded more like a cry.

"Those were the good old days, huh?" I was about to complain how things were so complicated now, between dirty diapers and mortgage payments, but I stopped with a pang of sadness. *He didn't even get to experience that. Being a dad. Owning a house. Getting married...*

"Well, anyway. I wish you were here." The weight in my chest lifted, slightly. I took the receiver away from my ear--

Sssssssshhhhh.

Something like a breath--a gust of wind, a whooshing sound--came from the phone. My heart dropped. I pushed it back against my ear.

"David?"

Silence.

Because of-fucking-course. People can't talk to the dead, ghosts don't exist, and this is all just pretend. My eyes burned and I swallowed, swallowing away the tears--

Click.

It was soft. Almost outside the range of my hearing. I pressed the phone so hard to my ear it hurt.

Click... Click-click... click...

It sounded like the clicking of a bad connection. Soft, barely audible, but there. My heart pounded in my chest as I listened to it with everything that I had. Not even breathing.

David? Could it really be? Maybe if Ouija boards talk to the dead, maybe if people visiting their loved one's graves get a whisper on the wind, maybe, just maybe, David could be on the other end for a fleeting moment--

"Sara."

The voice was a low, staticky growl.

Every muscle in my body froze. I opened my mouth but no sound came out. "...D-david?" I finally choked.

"*Sa...*" Static cut in, fuzzing out the rest of my name. Then a beat of silence. I held my breath, the receiver shaking against my ear. *Click... click-click.*

How is this happening? Maybe it was another one of my dreams. I pinched myself. Reached over and checked the time on my phone. Looked away, then back at the phone. Same time. Not a dream.

"David... is that really you?"

Click... click-click. A few seconds of static. *Click-click.* And then silence.

That's it. I lost the connection. I began to sob. All the memories came rushing back in colorful pieces. Proms and late nights and his laugh like melted chocolate. The conversations we had for hours, about life, philosophy, our future...

But then five words came over the line. Crystal clear. *"You should've never married William."*

He sounded so angry. None of his sweetness, none of his laughter. Just pure anger, compressed into a voice on the other end of the line. My entire body went cold. The receiver nearly slipped out of my hands.

"W-what?"

A fizzle of static. *Click-click-click.*

And then his voice again, cutting in and out. Despite the static, I understood him perfectly.

"*I—will—kill—you.*"

All the blood drained out of my face.

I stared out at the darkening garden. I was alone. The shadows under the foliage, they shifted with the wind in strange and horrifying ways. For a second I thought I could see the shadow of a tall young man, peeking out from behind the leaning trunk of a maple.

My nails dug into the metal shelf.

Ghosts, spirits... if you believed in that stuff... weren't they sometimes consumed by hatred? Didn't it eat up their entire being, until they became vengeful spirits? Hell-bent on punishing those who'd hurt them?

I swallowed.

"David, I'm so, so sorry," I whispered. "But... you're not here. I know we wanted to get married, but you left. What was I supposed to do? Be alone my whole life?"

He didn't have to answer.

I married one of his *friends*. He didn't need to tell me it was weird, that it was a betrayal, almost. But when William and I reconnected, everything just *clicked*. He wanted to be with me. He wanted to marry me. There was no waffling or rejection.

And I fell in love with him.

"David—" I started.

"*I—will—kill—you,*" he repeated.

Click-click. The connection became steadily clearer.

"*I—no—will—killed—you—out—*"

"*I—no—willya—illed—watch—out—*"

Click. And then, for just a moment, the connection was crystal clear.

"*I know William killed me. You watch out.*"

I dropped the receiver.

The accident. He'd lost his brakes driving home, coming down the mountain from Highpoint Park. After hanging out with some friends, one final hurrah before leaving for college.

One of them was William.

"David," I sobbed into the line. But it was useless. No sound came through on the other side. No clicks, no static, no voice.

Just silence.

CHRISTMAS TREE SHOPPING

Growing up, I never went Christmas tree shopping.

We had a fake tree from the '90s that sat in our basement, only to come out for an elaborate assembly ritual each year. Sorting through the 100+ plastic branches took hours, but it was something we were supposed to be grateful for. *Just be glad you're not out in the freezing weather, or trying to haul a fifty-pound tree up onto the roof of the car,* my mom would say.

When I moved into a place of my own, though, I decided to put an end to this nonsense. "We're going to get a *real* tree this year," I told my boyfriend, Robert.

We only had a 600-square-foot apartment, but I was determined. We'd get a tiny, skinny little thing to rival Charlie Brown's if we had to. So one December evening, we went over to the local farm to choose our tree.

I'd never been Christmas tree shopping before. But as soon as we arrived, I knew I'd love it. Precut trees were lined up in rows, each held upright by its own stand, spaced so close on the grass that they formed a dense forest. Edison light bulbs hung overhead, casting a warm golden glow. The weather was weird that evening—unseasonably warm and foggy—and the way the light dispersed through the fog, silhouetting the trees, looked like a shot from a Hallmark movie.

"This is *so cool,*" I whispered to Robert.

"Have you really never gotten a real tree before?"

"Yup, never. Hey, what's that?" I asked, pointing to the end of the field.

There was a large plastic roll of something, and standing next to it, a man. He looked very fitting here, with his flannel shirt and lumberjack beard.

"Netting they put on the trees, to keep all the branches in, so you can transport them more easily," he replied.

"Oooh. Cool." I took him by the arm. "Let's go find our tree!"

We started down one of the narrow aisles. The air smelled like pine—like that one candle Mom always burned around Christmastime. Robert tried to match my enthusiasm, but eventually seemed bored, lagging behind me as I ran through the place like an excited little girl.

I finally stopped in front of a particularly beautiful tree. Its branches were thick and lush, and the fragrance of pine was strong, filling my nose. Slowly, I reached out to touch it. The needles were surprisingly soft and pliable under my fingers—nothing like the shiny plastic ones I'd seen all my life.

"Robert, c'mere, I think I found—"

I stopped.

Robert wasn't behind me.

"Robert?"

I glanced around. But all I saw were the pine trees. Rows and rows of them, like a thick forest all around me. The lightbulbs buzzed above my head, their soft golden glow dispersing in the thick fog.

"Robert? Where are you?"

I hurried down the aisle, needles scraping at my jacket. *He couldn't have gone far.* Probably started looking at memes on his phone, and didn't even notice I was miles ahead of him. "Robert!" I called again.

No answer.

I pulled out my phone and shot off a text. *Where are you?* When no reply came, I sighed angrily and continued towards the rolly-netty things. Maybe he was waiting for me there.

But my sense of direction must've been messed up. Because when I rounded the corner, there were just more trees.

I pulled out my phone to call him—

And that's when I heard the footsteps.

Oh, thank goodness. I whipped around, trying to pinpoint the source. And then I saw it—a flash of motion between the trees.

It wasn't Robert.

It was the lumberjack-guy that I'd seen standing next to the netting. He was in the next aisle over. Slowly, methodically walking through the grass. As if looking for something.

Maybe I can ask him if he saw Robert.

I hurried down the aisle until I was several feet behind him, running parallel. I sucked in a breath—

And stopped dead.

Something was swinging from his hand. Something heavy, glinting gold in the lights strung above our heads.

An axe.

I stood frozen, watching him, until he turned the corner and disappeared among the trees. *Of course... of course he would have an axe. That's how they cut down the trees, right?* Nevermind that these trees had already been cut down. Maybe he needed to, I dunno, trim them or something. Maybe—

A scream echoed out on the other end of the field.

My heart plummeted. Instinctually, I lurched forward, to run towards the scream, to see if it was Robert—

Except I couldn't.

I looked down to see that the beltloop of my jeans was snagged on one of the needly branches. *Oh, come on.* I quickly reached down and unhooked it from my pants.

Then I took off running down the aisle.

But the aisle seemed so much narrower than before. I couldn't run that fast, with the branches reaching in from both sides, clawing at my legs. A corner lay up ahead and as I came up to it, I prayed I'd see the parking lot at the other end, with Robert waiting for me.

I didn't.

Ahead of me there were more trees. Like I was stuck

in some sort of Christmas tree maze, like they were rearranging themselves to block off all the exits. And the aisle was impossibly narrow now. I had to stop running so that I wouldn't trip over the branches extending into the path. The progress was slow but I kept going, leaping over branches, needles scratching at my face, snagging on my jacket.

And then I heard a sound.

It was coming off to my right. A sort of rolling sound, like a something round being turned over and over...

I ran over to the impossibly thick tangle of tree branches and peered out. More trees, but beyond them... I could see the checkout station, with the roll of netting for packing the trees.

The lumberjack man was there, packing something.

It wasn't a tree.

My stomach lurched as I saw what looked like a body being wrapped in white netting. A body wearing a black jacket and a striped hat...

I pushed myself through the hedge. The branches stabbed at me, scraping so hard against my arms that they drew blood. And then, finally, I popped out on the other side.

If the checkout station was there, I knew the parking lot was to the left. So I kept going, pushing myself through the tangled web of branches, until I was bloody and bruised on the other side.

I locked myself in the car and then I called 911.

By the time the police arrived, the man was gone. And Robert. Both had disappeared, and the patch of Christmas trees looked as magical as it did when we arrived.

The police have been searching for Robert for the past five days. Nothing has come up. No evidence, no clues, no body.

I know in my heart that he isn't with us anymore. His family is still holding onto hope, but I know what happened to him that day. But, sometimes, I wonder if there's a reason we haven't found his body yet.

Maybe he was put in that netting for a reason.

Maybe, that farm doesn't only sell trees.

THE SOUND ONLY MY WIFE CAN HEAR

A few months ago, my wife and I moved into a new house. It was everything we hoped for and more: a townhouse in a nice development, at a great price, and in great condition. The owner was an old widow with no kids or pets, and the thing looked brand new.

We were thrilled—until the noise started.

"Do you hear that?" she asked me one night, as we cooked dinner.

"Hear what?"

"That, like, really high-pitched noise."

I stopped stirring the sauce and listened. But all I could hear was the soft bubbling of our pasta water. "Sorry. I don't hear anything."

"Hmm," she said, scowling. "I don't hear it anymore, either."

But over the coming weeks and months, she heard it more. A high-pitched whine at all hours of the day and night. I told her maybe it was tinnitus. She insisted it wasn't—she heard it through both ears, and it just "sounded" like an external noise.

"Besides," she added. "I only hear it at home."

"Maybe you're hearing some electronic device through the wall." I remembered, as a kid in the '90s, my parents having a TV that made the most annoying sound. Even when it was on mute, I could hear that horrible high-pitched whine from two rooms over.

"Hmm... interesting," my wife replied, stirring her cup of coffee. "So you think... if the neighbors had some sort of electronic device... we'd hear it through the wall?"

"Maybe? We hear their dog all the time."

But, God, I wish I hadn't said anything. Because that afternoon, she came to me with the most batshit-insane theory I'd ever heard.

"They're doing it on purpose," she whispered—as if scared that they'd hear us. "They must've bought some device that makes an annoying sound, and they're purposely pointing it at us through the wall."

I nearly spit out my soda. "Uh, what now?"

"You know the Kowalskis hate us."

Okay, that part was true. We didn't have the best relationship with Jack and "Gigi" Kowalski. They hosted parties that went late. We threatened to call the cops once. Their dog pooped on our lawn sometimes. I'd lost my temper with Jack over it.

"Does a device like that even exist?" I asked.

But it did. "Noise stingers." A whole spread of them on NoiseMakersExpo for $49.99. I felt my gut turn as I read about them—people apparently did use them vindictively, to get back at neighbors. Sometimes they even caused health problems.

"Only someone totally demented would use this."

"Like the Kowalskis," she insisted.

"Well—"

"I'm going to go over there right now, and tell them if they don't turn off that thing—"

"Wait!" I held up my hands. "Let's not jump to conclusions. Uh, how about this? For the next week or so, let's just monitor it. See how often you hear it, try to figure out where exactly it's coming from. I'll listen for it too. And after that, if you're really convinced it's the Kowalskis, we'll go over and talk to them."

She huffed at me, but finally nodded. "Okay."

That night, at 3 AM, she gently woke me up. "I hear it," she whispered.

I forced myself awake. Our room was a mess of black and gray shadows and I rubbed my eyes, trying to orient myself. Then I strained my ears to listen.

But I didn't hear anything—other than the soft tinkle of the Kowalski's windchimes.

"I don't hear anything."

"It's really high-pitched. Maybe you're too old to hear it."

I scowled at her in the darkness. "I'm only three years older than you."

She got out of bed and walked over to each of the

four walls. "It's louder on this side," she said, gesturing to the south wall.

Confirmation bias, I thought to myself. *Of course she's going to think it's coming from the Kowalski's side.*

She slowly paced out of the room. I was so tired, but I forced myself out of bed too. She walked into the hallway, then into our guest bedroom. Shook her head, and started down the stairs.

By the time I caught up with her, she was going into the basement.

"Oh, for fuck's sake," I muttered.

When I got to the bottom she was standing at the south wall, near our utility closet, pressing her ear up against the cold cement.

"Jill, let's go back to—"

She immediately shushed me. "It's *right here,*" she whispered, her eyes wide. She motioned for me to come over.

I reluctantly put my ear against the wall. "I don't hear anything."

"Are you serious?"

I shook my head.

"It's so loud I can barely hear you."

"Yeah, but... they wouldn't put it in the basement. They'd put the noise stinger thing like, next to our bedroom or kitchen."

I wrapped my arm around her and gently guided her over to the stairs. Held her close, smiled at her, reassured her it was okay.

But inside, I was starting to doubt my wife's sanity.

Of course I wanted to believe my wife. But none of it made sense.

She heard a noise I couldn't hear. She claimed it was coming from the basement. And she insisted it was our neighbors, using some noise emitter against us.

"But I don't hear it," I told her that morning, as we drank our second cups of coffee.

"Your hearing is worse than mine."

I wasn't convinced, but then she opened her laptop and sat it in front of me. "I was trying to match the tone I heard last night, after you fell asleep. And I think it's around 17,000 Hz. Which is pretty hard to hear if you're in your 30s like us."

She typed 17,000 Hz into the search bar and played a video for me. And, I'll be damned, she was right. I didn't hear a thing. Curse all that listening to Pink Floyd in my youth.

So that should've been the end of it. She was hearing an electronic pitch that I couldn't. I should've believed her, taken her lead, and gone back to business as usual.

But I didn't.

The next time she heard the sound, at 5:47 PM, I surreptitiously pulled out my phone and hit 'record.' And after she went to sleep that night, I downloaded an the audio-editing program. I opened the file, and the proof was right there: instead of jagged blue lines showing soundwaves—

There was just a flat line.

I sat in the darkness in a cold sweat. There was no noise stinger, no vindictive plan by the Kowalskis, no noise coming through the basement wall.

It was all in her head.

What came next was one of the biggest fights in our marriage.

"I'm telling you. There *is* no noise!"

"What are you implying? That I'm making it up?!"

"No! But—look! I recorded it, and there's no sound!"

I opened my laptop and clicked on the audio program. Pulled up the recording. I zoomed in and showed her the flat line. "See? If there was sound, we'd *see* it."

"The phone probably just didn't pick it up."

She reached over and hit PLAY. And as the little marker moved through the flat line of silence, she grinned a triumphant grin at me. "I don't hear anything. You messed it up."

"Of course you don't hear anything, *now*."

She frowned at me. "What's that supposed to mean?"

"Power of suggestion. I told you there wasn't sound, I showed you the line, and so you don't hear anything. But in the middle of the night, in the scary basement, then of course you hear something."

Her face fell. "Wait a second." She pointed an accusatory finger at me. "Are you implying that I'm *imagining* the sound?"

"I mean... that's the only possibility left, Jill."

She stood up. Without a word, she stormed out of the kitchen and up the stairs. A second later, I heard our bedroom door slam shut.

The next day I apologized.

I knew I was right. I knew there was no sound. But choose your fights, right? This wasn't the hill I was going to die on. Jill was, and had always been, a wonderful wife to me. This wasn't worth our marriage.

But things got worse. Much worse.

Jill had continued logging every time she heard the sound in her notebook. But when I flipped through it the other day, I noticed it had shot up from about twice a day to more than ten.

A week ago, I walked into the kitchen to find her crouched on the floor. Hands pressed against her ears, frantically rocking back and forth. When I called out to her, she didn't even seem to hear me.

And then there was last night.

I woke up in the middle of the night to find the bed empty. I assumed Jill was in the bathroom, but then I noticed our door was open.

I went down the stairs, my heart pounding. "Jill?" I called out. "Jill, where are you?"

And then I heard it.

Not the high-pitched sound. But an awful, thumping sound, resonating through the house.

Coming from the basement.

I scrambled over to the basement door and wrenched it open. "Jill!" I shouted, running down the stairs. "Jill, are you—"

No.

She was standing in front of the wall. Repeatedly swinging a hammer into the concrete, into that one spot in the wall, near the utility closet, where she claimed the noise was coming from.

"Jill! Jill, what are you doing?"

Tears were streaming down her face. "Make it stop," she whimpered, as she lifted the hammer to swing again. "I have to... make it stop."

She lifted the hammer high above her head—

THWACK.

"Jill!" I ran over to her and grabbed the hammer out of her hands before she could swing it again. I thought for a moment she might try and wrestle it out of my arms, but she didn't. Instead, she collapsed in my arms, sobbing.

"I can't take it anymore," she whispered. "Please... make it stop."

That night, I took her to the ER. But the doctors—including the psychiatrist—couldn't find anything wrong with her. They insisted it was a form of tinnitus or Meniere's disease, and gave her some medication to help.

But the medication didn't help.

———

I was scared.

Seeing her slowly descend into madness was horrible. Seeing the woman I loved, the woman who was so strong and funny, crumbling into this shell of herself... turning into a prisoner of the noise in her head... it was a fate I wouldn't wish on anyone.

She stopped recording the times in her notebook. Just wrote *MAKE IT STOP,* over and over, in the spaces for each day. In handwriting that grew more frantic, more illegible, until it was just a mess of jagged scribbles.

I finally went over to the Kowalskis, soon after the ER visit. But even though they were kind of jerks, they seemed genuinely confused. I doubted they were actually the cause of the sound.

I tried to track down the previous owner, the widow, as well. In case there was something weird about this house, like some radioactive noise-emitting substance in the walls. But the number I found online repeatedly went to a generic voicemail message.

And then everything came crashing down.

I woke up with a start at 4 AM, dimly aware of a clanging noise downstairs. I shot out bed and rushed towards it, into the kitchen—

To find Jill standing there.

With a knife pointed at her ear.

She was crying, her face red, tears falling onto the counter. "I can't," she whimpered, the knife trembling in midair. "I can't do it. I can't listen to it anymore."

"Jill—please. Put the knife down."

"I hear it all the time," she said, her eyes locked on mine. "And the longer I hear it... I think I hear other things, too. Mixed in with the sound." She lowered her voice to a whisper. "It sounds like screaming."

Her hand tensed—

I leapt for her, and in a nick of time, shoved her hand away from her head. The knife went flying, falling on the tile with a resounding clatter.

I held her as she sobbed into my shoulder.

It's been five years.

Jill had to spend a few nights in the hospital, on watch for self-harm. After that, she spent months in intensive therapy while I scoured the housing market for a new place. We eventually found something that wasn't nearly as nice as the place we had, and fifty thousand dollars more.

But when we moved in, I knew it was worth it. Almost immediately, Jill's symptoms started to get better. She told me she didn't hear any weird noises. She started smiling again.

I thought the nightmare was over.

But then, one day, I got a call from Jack Kowalski, of all people.

"Rich, you're not going to believe it," he breathed into the phone.

"What?"

"The new owners of your unit. They were putting in some plumbing, in the basement. They had to take apart some of the wall and..." He sucked in a shaking breath. "They found something."

My heart plummeted.

"They found a body, Rich. The body of a young woman. They think she's been there since the foundation was poured."

The phone clattered to the floor.

I could hear Jack's muffled voice coming from the speaker. Going on and on about how they found it. How they thought it belonged to a woman who went missing in the area a while back, when the houses were being built.

But I couldn't concentrate. Couldn't think. All I could do was stare at the wall, the room spinning around me. Imagining the sound that my wife heard, all hours of the day and night.

And how she insisted that it was coming from the basement.

THE BANK DEPOSITS

The first deposit came on a Tuesday.

I was on my way to lunch when my phone vibrated in my pocket. **Woo-hoo! You just got paid!** my budgeting app gleefully told me. *That's odd,* I thought. Payday wasn't until Friday.

I opened the app—to find a deposit of $250.

It was from a sender I didn't recognize. "AWST-GHY2276". I quickly shot off a text to my husband (it was our joint account,) but he didn't recognize it either. My next thought was PayPal; I did occasionally get weird payments (I have a crafting side hustle that's more of a side crawl), but those payments usually say "PayPal" in the transaction.

So who was just... giving me money?

It must be a scam.

But as the hours went by, I didn't get any weird texts or phone calls. That fat $250 just sat there in my bank account, taking up space.

"We should give it back," my husband said, when I got home.

"I don't think we can do that."

"Sure we can. We call the bank, tell them to reverse the transaction."

I shot him a look. "Or, we could just... keep it. Someone *did* give it to us."

"That's unethical."

"What's unethical is forcing the kids to eat rice and beans for lunch every day." I slammed the refrigerator shut and plopped down on the couch. "Look, I feel a little weird about it too, okay? But it's not like I picked up a wallet someone dropped and found $250 in it. Someone actually *gave* this to us, whether it was accidental or not."

We argued about it until we went to sleep. Well, not really *argued,* more just aggressively talked at each other. With three kids and two full-time jobs, neither of us had the energy to properly argue anymore.

When I woke up the next morning, there was a text from an Unknown Number waiting for me.

At 2:13 PM today, go to the corner of 12th Ave. and North St. Take a photo of the short man in the black coat.

"What the heck?"

But Jerry had already left for work. I'd tell him about it later. The weird text from a wrong number. As I got the kids ready for school, I couldn't stop smiling. "Tomorrow, you guys are going to get a *special* lunch. Not rice and beans. Something really good," I told them as we walked down the driveway. After waving to them on the bus, I left for work.

But then another text came in, as I was riding the elevator up.

If you want to keep the $250, take the photo.

My throat went dry.

It wasn't free money. Some... some weirdo wired $250 to me. The elevator doors slid open and I stumbled out. *How do they have my number? Is it someone I know?* I glanced around at the hall of cubicles, at the people I'd worked side-by-side with for five years. *Ed. Ed is weird enough to pull some shit like this.* But then I frowned. *If Ed were wiring me $250, he would be asking for a photo of... something else.*

I set my phone face down on the desk, and got to work.

I didn't spend another thought on the text. I pretended it didn't even happen. I just focused on my happy little spreadsheets, on the upcoming presentation, and hoped it would all go away by five.

It didn't.

At 2 o'clock sharp, my phone buzzed loudly. And when I pulled up the text, my breath caught in my throat.

Why haven't you left yet?

I glanced wildly around the office. But nobody was looking at me. I ran over to the window. The sidewalk below was filled with people, but none of them were looking up in my direction.

Fear pounded through my veins.

Bzzt.

You want to give your kids that special lunch tomorrow, don't you?

I froze.

No.

They'd been in my yard. Watching me. And now they were somewhere on the street, or *in this very office,* watching my every move—

I shot up from the desk and ran to the elevator.

It took me eight minutes to get to the corner of 12th and North. Running, in heels. Panting, I glanced around at my surroundings—but I didn't see anything out of place. A woman jogging by; a mother pushing a stroller; two businessmen arguing as they crossed the street.

And at 2:13... a short man in a black coat strolled into view.

He pressed the button for the crosswalk. Quickly, I whipped out my phone—pretended I was texting—and snapped a photo of him.

I rushed back to the office building, tears stinging my eyes as my fingers slid across the screen. **Here's your photo,** I texted, with the image. **Now leave me the fuck alone.**

After work I went to the grocery store. I got my kids organic sliced turkey and aged gouda and fucking gourmet Swiss chocolate for lunch tomorrow. I'd played their stupid little sick game, and dammit if I wasn't going to reap the rewards.

As the good approached the conveyor belt, my phone vibrated.

Woo-hoo! You just got paid!

My heart fell into my stomach.

And it fell through the floor when I saw the amount.

$1,000.

Whatever they were going to ask me to do tomorrow... I had a feeling it was going to be a lot worse than taking a photo of some random guy.

I threw my groceries into the trunk of the car, the whole world going blurry with my tears. *Just ignore it. Whatever they ask you to do tomorrow... just don't respond. They'll take the money back and that'll be it. Then you can go to the police and tell them everything.*

But I was naïve to assume they'd wait until tomorrow. Because as I started the car, my phone buzzed again.

Drive to the pier.

I stared at those four words, my heart pounding in my chest.

And then I leapt into action. **I DON'T WANT TO PLAY YOUR SICK FUCKING GAME,** I texted, my hands shaking. **TAKE YOUR MONEY BACK. I DON'T WANT IT. LEAVE ME ALONE!**

Brzzt.

It's too late for that.

I swallowed. **What do you mean, it's too late?** I wrote back. Three dots popped up, showing they were typing...

And then the message appeared.

Because the cargo is already in your backseat.

My heart pounded in my ears.

You really shouldn't leave your car unlocked, Lynn.

I closed out of the texting app. Pulled up the phone and began dialing 9-1—

Something *thumped* against the back of my seat.

Every muscle in my body froze. I held my breath. The shadows in the rearview mirror shifted, but I couldn't quite make out—

Brzzt.

Drive to the pier, and you'll be safe.

But if you call the police...

They didn't need to finish that sentence.

I swung out of the parking lot and drove as fast as I could to the pier. When I got there, I parked in a dark little corner and cut the lights. Now in the darkness, in the silence, I could hear them breathing. A steady rush of air, right behind my ear.

Brzzt.

Close your eyes.

I squeezed them shut tight. Rustling movement in the backseat; and then the open and close of a car door. Faint footsteps on the pavement, receding into the darkness.

I let out the breath I'd been holding.

I don't know how long I'd been sitting there with my eyes closed, but I finally felt like it was safe to open them when I hadn't heard the footsteps in a long time. I sobbed as I drove home, so thankful I was alive. Praying that this whole nightmare was over. That whoever this person was, they'd used me as much as they could and would move on to the next poor soul.

But I wasn't so lucky.

Because this morning, when I woke up, I had a new notification.

Woo-hoo! You just got paid!

The amount?

$10,000.

I called in sick to work. All I could do was sit there, staring at my phone, my heart pounding in my chest. I couldn't eat. Couldn't focus. Couldn't *move*. Because I knew, sooner or later, I'd get the instructions.

It was almost noon when my phone pinged. Hands shaking, I picked it up and stared at the message.

Deliver the package to 12 Maple Avenue.

Package? What pack—

Ding.

The doorbell rang—followed by a dull *thump* on the porch.

No. No, no, no. The kitchen swam beneath me. Slowly, I forced myself up; then I walked to the door and swung it open.

At my feet, there was a brown box.

It wasn't that small. About a foot on a side. Heart pounding in my chest, I reached down and picked it up. It was heavier than I expected, but not exceedingly so. Taking deep breaths, I started back inside—

I stopped.

There was a pool of dark liquid where the box had just been.

I lifted the box up and saw, in the center, the cardboard was wet. Soggy. Stained dark red...

I dropped the box and screamed. It made a wet *thwack* on my front porch. I leapt inside and slammed the door—

Brzzt.

My phone. On the kitchen table.

The screen lit up with a message. I slowly walked towards it, the pain building in my chest.

Deliver the package, Lynn.

I texted back, my fingers flying over the screen. **FUCK OFF. YOU'RE SICK. I'M CALLING THE POLICE!**

The reply came back almost instantly.

You'll be dead before you get the chance.

I whipped around. And then I saw it: on the other side of the street, a black sedan with dark windows idled by the curb. My throat went dry. If they were holding a gun...

They'd have a straight shot at my head.

I ran into the living room and ducked behind the couch. No one could possibly see me, through any windows. Hands shaking, I raised my thumb over the dial button—

Brzzt.

We have a second car at JCP Elementary. It's recess. All I have to do is give the word.

My throat went dry. All the air sucked out my lungs. I couldn't breathe. **Please,** I typed back, **please just leave us alone.**

The reply popped up.

I will, if you deliver the package. This is your final task.

I got up. Slowly walked into the kitchen. Through the window I could see the brown box, askew on the steps. The wet, darkened stain.

And please, don't drop it again. It's fragile.

Shaking, I made my way back to the door. I picked up the box. Something *thunked* against the side as I rotated it in my hands. I swallowed and tried not to imagine what was inside.

I stiffly walked to the car. Put the box into the passenger seat. Then I got in the driver's seat and stared out the windshield.

I can't do this.

But when I glanced in the rearview mirror, I saw the black car. Idling at the curb. Watching me.

As I drove, I couldn't stop glancing at the box. At the dark red seeping into the gray cloth of the passenger seat. Deep down, I think I knew what was in the box. But that didn't stop me from pulling over to the side of the road, just outside of town, and taking a peek.

My hands shook as I pulled off the tape. As soon as the seal was broken, a horrible smell filled the car. Gasping, I grabbed the flap and quickly pulled it up—

And immediately vomited.

It was a head.

The head of an adult man.

I grabbed the flaps and pushed them shut. Grabbed the tape off the floor and quickly sealed the box again. Rolled the windows down to get rid of the smell. Gasped in gulps of fresh air.

Because in the quick flash I'd seen, the face looked familiar.

It looked like the man I'd taken a photo of, in the black coat.

I hit the gas and sped through town, until I was turning into Oak Grove—the community of McMansions built several years back. I passed brick archways, white columns, sprawling lawns of green. I frantically looked for the number 12.

And then I found it.

The house was grand, sitting on top of a hill. White columns stretched up to the sky, and a large window reflected the clear blue sky. I pulled up to the curb and grabbed the box.

Then I burst out and ran up to the front door.

I could hear the *thump-thump-thump* of the head rattling inside with each step. A wave of nausea hit me, but I forced myself to concentrate on my steps. *Almost there. Almost.* As soon as my feet hit the porch, I dropped the box and got the hell out. When I was halfway down the hill I heard the door creak open behind me—then a pause—and then a woman's scream.

I kept running. Dove into the car. Hit the gas and peeled down the road.

When I was finally back in my house, every door locked and sealed, I sent off a final text.

I delivered the box. Our transactions are over. Never contact me again.

I stared at the screen, my eyes watering. And then three little dots popped up.

You weren't supposed to open the box, Lynn.

The phone slipped out of my hands. And then I began to sob. My entire body shook as I imagined what horrible things this person would ask me to do next. Knowing that I was powerless, that they knew where I lived, where my kids went to school.

But it's been a month now, and I haven't heard anything.

I've been watching the news closely. I learned the man who died was a local businessman—a corrupt one, who'd embezzled quite a bit of money. He had so many enemies, the police didn't even know where to start. They never traced anything back to me—or, presumably, the person who'd been texting me.

Then last night happened.

There'd been a break in the case, according to the news broadcast. A break that police were confident would lead them to the killer—and any accomplices.

They found the murder weapon.

Buried in some muck in the water, next to the pier.

MY GRANDMA IS ACTING ODD

I moved in with my grandma about a year ago. Some people think it's dorky for a 21-year-old to live with her grandma, but I love it. She's the best roommate—never complains, even when I have people over or stink up the kitchen with a cooking experiment. The rent's cheap, and in return I cook for her, drive her around, etc. We're really close too—she's kind, has a sharp sense of humor, and can entertain me for hours with tales from her childhood in Italy.

But then things started to change.

On Wednesday evening, I needed some scissors. They weren't in the usual place, so I went upstairs to Grandma's room, where she sews sometimes.

But just as my hand touched the doorknob, she came flying up the stairs.

"What are you doing?"

"Are the scissors in your room?"

"Don't go in my room!"

She glared at me as I made my way back downstairs. *That was... weird. She'd never told me to stay out of her room before.*

And the trend only continued. She started to become more reclusive, more private. Closing herself off to me. When she didn't eat dinner with me two days in a row, I made her favorite—chicken and wild rice. But all she said was "Sorry, dear, I'm full," before disappearing up the stairs.

"How could she be full?" I grumbled to myself, as I spooned the leftovers into a Tupperware. "I haven't seen her eat anything tonight."

I told my mom I was starting to worry. But she didn't seem concerned. "Older people sometimes change. Grandma's almost 90, and well... she knows it's going to be her time soon. Sometimes people get depressed, or bitter, or just *different*. Your grandpa definitely did."

But I couldn't stop the horrible feeling in the pit of my stomach, that there was just something... *wrong*.

As the days went on, the feeling continued to grow.

On Saturday morning, our neighbor stopped by to ask if we could get his mail while he was away. As he stood there on the porch with his big German Shepherd, my Grandma started down the stairs.

The dog began to growl.

Not just a little growl. Hackles up, teeth bared, the whole nine yards. "Woah, easy, Teton," our neighbor said, backing away.

Rrrrrooof!

"I'd better go," he said sheepishly. But as he ran down the driveway, the dog kept glancing back at us, barking.

"What did he want?" Grandma asked behind me.

I jumped. She was *right* behind me—and somehow I hadn't heard her creep up. "Uh, we have to get his mail for a few days," I replied, closing the door. "That's okay. Right?"

She just shrugged and walked away.

Things continued to get worse. I'd wake up in the middle of the night and hear her footsteps out in the hallway. Back and forth, back and forth. I had half a mind to think the place was haunted—until I opened my door a crack and saw her figure, clothed in her floral nightgown, walking back and forth.

Once, when class was canceled and she didn't know I was home, I heard her crying upstairs. I peeked around the corner to see her standing in front of my bedroom door, her face hiding in her hands. "Grandma?" I called. But she simply shook her head and ran into her bedroom.

And then there was the smell.

Now when I went upstairs, this horrible stench hit me. A rotting, decaying smell. Like someone had left a plate of raw meat out for days.

And as I sniffed around, I realized it was coming

from Grandma's room. But when I turned the knob—the door was locked.

"Grandma... have you noticed it, uh, kinda smells up there? Did you leave some food out, maybe?"

Her eyes went wide when I asked her. Then—suddenly—without a word she bolted up the stairs and slammed the door to her room shut.

And that was when I decided to take action.

Something terrible was going on here—and I was going to find out what.

Three days later, the package came. I greedily ripped it open and shook out the contents.

A long, thin key. Designed to fit into the holes in home doorknobs and unlock them from the outside.

I crept up the stairs, even though I knew Grandma was watching TV with the volume full blast. Then I crouched in front of her door and slid the key into the hole.

After a few minutes of fumbling, I heard the *click*.

I pushed the door open.

The stench hit me like a truck. Fetid, sour decay that made me want to vomit. I frantically waved it away—and then I saw what was on the bed.

No.

A body. Blue-skinned, stiff, lifeless. One arm hanging over the side of the bed, white fingers dangling towards the ground.

Not just any body.

My *Grandma's*.

A soft sound came from behind me. "I'm so sorry, dear," my Grandma's voice whispered in my ear.

But when I turned around, the hallway was empty.

I LEFT MY RECORDING APP ON LAST NIGHT

Last night before bed, I dictated some notes about a project I'm working on into my voice recording app. When I got up in the morning, I realized I'd never turned it off; there was a seven-hour, twenty-one minute long recording waiting for me.

Later that night, as I was cooking dinner, I decided to have a listen. Did I still snore? Two years ago, in my last serious relationship, my boyfriend said I did. Or did I sleepwalk? One time I found my salt in the middle of the counter, without any memory of putting it there. Maybe I was one of those people who could cook a whole meal in their sleep without ever knowing about it.

Curious, I tapped a random spot in the middle of the seven hours and hit 'PLAY.'

Quiet white noise played through the phone's speakers. Then the soft rustling of blankets, as I rolled over.

I finished cooking my chicken, pulled the Brussels sprouts out of the toaster oven, and plated everything up. I ate for several minutes, listening, but there was only more white noise. *Maybe I should just put on the TV. This is getting a little boring.*

But just as I reached for the phone, I heard it.

Creeeaaak.

The unmistakable sound of a door opening.

Huh. I don't remember getting up to use the bathroom. Knife poised over the chicken breast, I listened closely, for footsteps or a toilet flush or anything else. A moment later, I heard the door quietly shut; then there was only more white noise.

I shrugged and cut into the chicken. Took a bite. *Too dry. I'll have to brine it longer next time.* I lifted my fork over a roasted sprout—

I froze.

There was a sound coming over the white noise. So quiet it was almost inaudible. But I could hear it, because it was irregular—a *sshhh*ing or hissing noise coming through at odd intervals. I paused, tilting my head, holding my breath as I listened.

The sound grew louder. I turned the volume up on my phone, holding my breath, straining to listen. I couldn't quite make it out... but it almost sounded like...

Whispering.

The sound then faded away, and the uninterrupted rush of the white noise took over. I let out the breath I'd been holding and slumped back in my seat.

I listened for the next several minutes as I finished dinner, but it was just more white noise and rustling. *I*

guess I don't snore anymore, I thought. I picked up my plates and got up to bring them to the sink—
And then I heard it.
Shabantemetashabantemeta
Whispering.
Loud whispering.
As if, whoever was saying it, was right next to the phone.
As if they were *right in my bed*.
I dropped the plate. It shattered on the floor. But I couldn't move. Couldn't breathe.
No. It has to be me. I must be sleeptalking.
There's no way it could be someone else.
I collapsed back into the chair and stared at the phone. At the jagged soundwave on the app. The whispering continued, a string of indecipherable syllables.
And then it stopped. I grabbed the phone and rewound it, playing the whisper again. But I couldn't make out any individual words. Just the same sounds over and over: *shabantemeta, shabantemeta.*
What was I trying to say?
I paused the recording and whispered the syllables to myself. *Shabantemeta.* But I had to admit... the way I whispered them didn't sound at all like the recording.
Was someone... actually in here?
Should I call the police?
I shook my head. I'd watched too many true crime shows. There was absolutely no evidence of a break-in. I locked the place up like a fortress at night. It had to just be me, sleeptalking. My mom told me I sleeptalked once

or twice as a kid. I must do it all the time, without realizing.

Sighing, I finally got up and cleaned the shattered plate.

That evening, as I went about various chores, I kept the recording playing in the background. I thought I heard the whispering a few more times—but it was so quiet, it very well could've been my imagination. Other than that, there was just white noise and occasional rustling. Finally, at around ten PM, I reached the end.

I got settled in bed, pulling the covers over me. For a second, I considered turning the app on and recording my sleep again; but I decided against it. It would only bring more stress. So I cuddled against the pillow and closed my eyes.

But as I drifted off into sleep, a horrible thought occurred to me.

Before the whispering, I'd heard the door open and close.
But I didn't hear it a second time.
If it wasn't me, whoever it was—
They're still here.

MATRYOSHKA DOLL

Working in a pawn shop, we get all kinds of weird shit. But there's one thing they all have in common: their condition. Dresses are stained, handbags are ripped, even jewelry is wonky and bent.

That's what made the matryoshka doll so special: she was in perfect condition.

I found her while sorting through Wednesday's sales. As soon as I saw her, I gasped. Almond-colored wood, finely carved into a peanut shape. A beautiful face, painted more photorealistically than other matryoshka dolls I'd seen. Sparkling blue eyes and rosy cheeks, with a colorful scarf tying up her black hair.

I set her on the table, with the other goods destined for the back of the shop. But then, my curiosity got the better of me. I picked her back up and—*pop!*—twisted her open.

An identical doll stared back up at me, just a little bit smaller. Rosy cheeks, pretty blue eyes, pink and white flowers painted on her dress. I took her out of the bottom shell and—

Pop!

Inside, another doll stared back up at me.

Except this one wasn't identical.

It was *nearly* identical. But the woman's mouth was open this time, in a little O. Her hands were unclasped, as well, and hanging at her sides.

Huh. I thought they were all supposed to look the same. I'd seen some matryoshka dolls that made changes to the woman's dress—different flowers or patterns—with each iteration. But the woman's face usually appeared identical.

I twisted her open again. *Pop.*

The woman's mouth was open wider. Her eyes were wider too—the black strokes of her eyelids bulging out from the previous almond shape. Her elbows were bent and her hands were moving up, towards her face.

I paused, glancing from this doll to the other three.

Pop.

I froze.

The fifth doll's mouth was open wide. As if she were screaming. Her eyes were so wide they were nearly perfect circles.

And her hands were held out in front of her body... as if she were trying to defend herself.

I sat there for a long time, staring at that painted face. This was starting to feel like some sort of joke. Someone trying to scare me. Come to think of it, the matryoshka doll didn't look that different from me. Black hair, blue eyes.

Is this supposed to be some sort of threat?

I shook my head. Sighing, I twisted the doll open again—

And it clattered to the floor.

The woman's face was covered in blood. Dark red painted in meticulous lines down the side of her face. It dripped off of her face and onto her dress, staining the pink flowers red.

When I picked it up, I felt a deep scratch in the wood —on the back of her head.

I felt sick. I set the doll down on the table and took a deep breath. *I'll get here early, finish inventory in the morning.* It was almost ten o'clock and there was no way I was going to stay here another second with this creepy-ass doll.

But as I began to stand, my curiosity again got the better of me. I snatched the doll off the table and pulled her apart again.

Pop.

My blood ran cold.

The doll looked similar to the previous one. Blood dripping down her face, onto her dress. Mouth hanging open in a silent scream.

Except, in this one, her eyes were closed.

And her skin was so pale it was almost blue.

My heart pounded in my ears. Hands shaking, I pulled at the ends of the doll. My hands slipped against the wood. But on the third try, I finally got the doll open.

There wasn't a doll inside.

Instead, there was a folded piece of paper.

I was shaking like a leaf. But I pulled the paper out of the doll and unfolded it, little black dots dancing at the edge of my vision.

Four little words, written in sloppy scrawl.

I'll see you soon.

I ran out of the pawn shop. I thought I heard the distinctive *thump* of footsteps behind me—but I dove into my car without looking back. When I got to my apartment I drew the deadbolt and collapsed onto the floor, sobbing.

The police haven't been able to find who did this. My boss remembers the man who sold it to us, but his description matches nearly every white, brown-haired guy in America. The name he used was fake, and we don't have security cameras.

He's untraceable.

I quit my job and moved to a new apartment. But other than that, I don't know what to do. Part of me thinks that, since nothing has happened in months, he's moved on.

But then I have the nightmares.

Nightmares of being crammed into a life-sized matryoshka doll. The wood closing in like a coffin, the sliver of light at my waist getting narrower by the second. Then—*pop!*—the wooden ends meet and I'm scratching at the wood, screaming for help, my mouth open in an *O* like the painted face of the doll.

But nobody can hear me.

WATER TORTURE

WATCH ME TRY CHINESE WATER TORTURE—WILL I FALL INTO PSYCHOSIS!?!

Yeah. You read that right. I'm a content creator and I decided to drip water on my head for 5 hours, and livestream the entire thing.

The things we do for money, huh?

"My friend Leslie here has restrained me," I said into the camera, as the dripper hovered above me. "My hands are handcuffed behind my back, my ankles are strapped to the chair, and I am completely unable to move."

Leslie gave an awkward thumbs-up at the camera.

"Did you know Chinese water torture didn't originate in China? The earliest account is from 15th century Italy. There's also a kinda creepy drawing from Sweden with it. Leslie, can you hold that up for them?"

She held up the drawing I'd printed out from Wikipedia, of a murderer screaming as water dripped onto his head. I grinned into the camera.

"Apparently, if you do this long enough, you start hallucinating. 10 hours, and you go into psychosis. I don't believe it. But we'll find out, won't we? Leslie, do the honors?"

She reached up and turned the knob.

A second later I felt a cold, fat drop of water fall onto my scalp.

-

"One hour has elapsed," I said, looking into the camera I'd placed across the room. "I feel... mostly good. The water was really annoying at first, but I've gotten used to it. I just wish I could dry off my face. And get out of these handcuffs."

The metal was biting into my wrists and my left hand was asleep. But I was stuck—like an idiot, I had no backup plan.

I had to wait for Leslie. Four hours to go.

-

"Hour 2. This sucks." I nodded to my sweatshirt, which was soaked. "I'm tired. I'm cold. And—" *Drip.* Another drop of water hit me on the head, oozing into my hair.

"The dripping isn't at regular intervals, and it's driving me *crazy*. I never know when they next one's coming. Sometimes it drips out one, then another right after. Sometimes it waits several minutes between drips. Sometimes I hear this little gurgling noise beforehand, and then I try to get ready for it, but somehow that makes it worse, you know?"

This still wasn't as bad as the Frosting Challenge I did last year (don't ask), but it was starting to become very un-fun. I leaned forward, as much as my restraints would allow, and rested my head on the kitchen table.

A drop of cold water fell onto the base of my neck—and slowly made its way down my spine.

Maybe Dad was right. Maybe, it was time for me to get a "real" job.

"Three hours."

I was cold. My wrists stung. And there was this pressure in my chest, a ball of anxiety, as I waited for that next godforsaken drop of water to hit me.

It was stupid—logically, I knew that. It was just water. But the repetition, and the irregularity of it. It was like listening to a ticking clock. A *broken* clock, out of rhythm, out of sync. *Tiktik-tock. Tocktick... TICK.* Sometimes I heard a soft gurgling sound and my entire body would seize up. When the drop didn't come, I relaxed. Only for a big fat one to hit me square on the head and slowly, ever-so-slowly trickle down my face.

Then it would bead there, sticking to my chin, for what felt like hours until finally breaking free and splattering onto my already-soaked sweatshirt.

"I'm not hallucinating or anything," I said. "But I'm

really stressed out. I can't remember the last time I was this stressed." I closed my eyes and let out an anguished sigh.

And then I remembered.

I was handcuffed to the chair... but I didn't need my hands to make a call.

"Hey Google," I shouted in the direction of my phone, sitting on the kitchen counter. "Call Leslie."

She picked up after two rings. "Hey, Charlie? Everything okay?"

Relief flooded me. Suddenly the handcuffs didn't hurt so much; the water dripping onto my face barely made me flinch. "Yeah. Sort of. I think I'm done with this water torture thing."

"Oh, already? It's that miserable, huh?"

"Yeah. I'm freezing and sore and I just don't think I can keep this up much longer." *Drip*—this one hit me on my cheek, and slowly traveled down my neck like an icy finger. "Can you come over and untie me?"

"I'm afraid I can't do that."

My stomach dropped. "Uh, what?" I asked, with a nervous laugh. "Why not?"

Silence.

"Leslie?"

A pause.

Had the call disconnected? I glanced at the counter— My phone wasn't there.

What the... But then I remembered. Before setting up for the water torture, I'd left my phone charging upstairs. There's no way I'd actually talked to Leslie just now.

I have to get out of here.

I violently rocked my body back and forth, trying to move the chair underneath me. If I could just get my chair a foot backwards, I'd be out of the water's range. With a grunt, I lurched.

But the chair barely budged.

-

Three and a half hours.

I sat completely frozen in the chair. Drops of water slowly slid down my cheeks and onto my sweater, but I didn't even blink. I wouldn't let it get to me. *Drip*—another drop—the 107th one since the hallucination. I'd been counting them to keep my concentration, and it was working. *Gurgle—here comes 108—*

Creeeeeeaaaak.

I froze, staring towards the hallway.

But no sounds followed. I let out the breath I'd been holding and closed my eyes, trying to calm myself. Breathe in, breathe out. *In less than two hours, Leslie will be here. I just have to make it until then—*

Something cold poked against my spine.

I froze as it slowly, carefully, made its way up my back. Tears burned my eyes as I resisted the urge to turn around. *It's not real. It's not real.*

But it felt real.

In my research of water torture I'd read about an artist in New Zealand, who'd done it as part of some art exhibit. In the final hours she said she felt the presence of her dead husband, stroking his finger up and down her back.

But the cold finger slowly moving up my spine did not feel loving. I began to sob as it passed my shoulderblades, heading towards my neck.

Drip.

Almost four hours.

I heard a child laughing softly, just beyond my view in the hallway. Little pattering footsteps across the wooden floor. But when I finally saw a glimpse of it, there was something horribly off with the way it moved. Like it was something inhuman, trying to imitate human movement.

Drip.

Something was walking behind me. I could see its shadow passing over me, stretched out on the tile floor. Cold fingers grazed my spine again, and this time when the fingers reached my neck... they squeezed.

Drip.

And then the most horrible one. The last one I remembered, before everything went black.

The voice started off soft, barely audible. But I recognized it instantly: my mother's voice. She was singing Brahm's lullaby, which she used to sing to me as a child.

Before she died, 14 years ago.

The lullaby got louder as I sat strapped to the chair, frozen. *Pleasant dreams until the dawn...* The sound moved around the house, sometimes coming from out in the hallway, sometimes from upstairs. Tears ran down my face as I listened to her sing. *Start the day, with a smile...*

Drip.

Her voice was right in my ear.

I screamed. I began rocking the chair back and forth, violently. Trying to desperately escape. But the chair barely moved—

Drip.

She was standing in front of me.

I stared at her baby blue slippers on my tile floor. My gaze slowly went up... across her white nightgown... towards the face I hadn't seen in 14 years—

—

I woke up in the hospital.

Leslie's face hung over mine, her eyes red and swollen from crying. "I was so worried about you. I thought—I thought we'd lost you..."

That night, after I returned home, I watched a replay of the livestream. I fastforwarded to the last thing I remember—around four hours into the video.

I could see myself sitting on the chair. The dripper hanging above me. I watched myself scream, as I heard my mother's voice in my ear. Then I saw my eyes slowly travel upwards... and stop about five feet off the ground, where her face would be.

Then I violently turned away—

And began bashing my head into the kitchen table.

After several sickening *thwacks,* I could see the blood. Thick patches blooming out of my hair, running down my face. But I didn't stop. If anything, I sped up, wildly thrashing my head into the table as hard as I possibly could—

And then my entire body went still.

I'd knocked myself unconscious.

I watched in horror as I lay there, eyes closed, blood pooling out onto the table. No wonder Leslie had thought I was dead. Several minutes went by, and then I saw her run into the frame, frantically tending to me.

But then I saw something else.

Just for a second. In the water pooled on the floor. A dark shape, flitting across the reflections—then vanishing from sight.

Maybe there is more to water torture than we thought.

MY BASEMENT FELL INTO AN ABANDONED MINE

Last year, my husband and I bought a house. It was pretty cheap, on account of it being pretty small and off the beaten track. We thought we'd gotten a good deal—until the basement caved in.

It happened in the middle of the night. I woke up at 3:30 AM to a loud crash that caused the windows to rattle. Terrified that someone had broken in, my husband Roger and I grabbed our mace and combed the entire house.

It was Roger who found it first.

"Diane!"

I found him standing at the top of the stairs, looking pale. He pointed down—to where our basement floor was simply... gone.

"What the fuck?" I whispered.

Both of us were too scared to go down the stairs. But upon closer inspection we noticed it was really only half the floor missing. The area behind and around the stairs seemed intact, while beyond the stairs was a huge hole that seemed to go down at least ten feet. We couldn't see the bottom from the dim light the basement bulbs cast.

The next few hours after that were devoted to frantically calling our home insurance and having the police/fire department come. They told us this had actually happened a few times before in our area. Apparently a lot of smaller mines here went unregistered during copper mining in the 1600s. People just built homes over them without even knowing.

While I'm thankful for their help, the firemen and police officers were honestly a little rude. They immediately cordoned off the basement and wouldn't let us get anywhere near it. "It's really dangerous," they said—but that didn't stop *them* from going into the basement. They were down there for hours.

Insurance would most likely cover the repairs, but the house would be unsafe to live in until it was fixed. Thankfully our elderly neighbor, Gertrude, offered for us to stay with her. "I could use some help around here, anyway," she said with a smile.

It was almost midnight when we got into bed, exhausted from a day of moving and calling contractors. But just as I pulled the covers over me, I realized—

"Shit. I forgot my rings."

I don't sleep with my engagement or wedding ring on. And in the chaos of everything, I forgot to bring them over.

"Rings?"

"My engagement and wedding ring. They're still on the nightstand!"

"You can get them tomorrow," Roger grumbled.

"What if the house collapses before then?"

"It won't."

"I'll just go over there quickly and get them."

"*Now?*"

I nodded. Then I got out of bed, pulled on my jeans, and started downstairs.

The house was quiet. Gertrude had already gone to sleep. I snuck out as quietly as I could, then raced across her lawn and into ours. Ran up the porch steps, pushed the key into the lock, and swung the door open.

The house was completely silent. Still. Dark. It was weird seeing everything so... empty. I mean, I'd arrived to an empty house before, but not in the middle of the night like this.

I flicked on the light and went upstairs.

I walked into the bedroom, grabbed the rings off the nightstand, and turned around. Started for the stairs—

Creeeeaaaak.

I froze.

Is someone in the house? I glanced around, clutching the rings to my chest. Then my eyes locked on the front door. *I'll run down the stairs and out the door. They won't get me. They won't—*

Creeeaaak.

I whipped around.

It was the bedroom door. *I was just in there. No one's in there.* I frowned, watching as it pushed open another inch—*creeeeeaaaak*—and then stopped.

There was a draft coming from somewhere.

I went downstairs and looked around—and immediately noticed the problem.

The basement door was open.

One of the firemen must've left it open. I walked towards it, slowly. Even though I knew it was just a simple mistake, my heart was hammering in my chest. I grabbed the edge of the door and started to push it closed—

Drip.

The sound was soft. Like a tiny drop of water falling from our basement and hitting the floor of the mine below. Unable to stop myself, I turned to look down.

The stairs descended into the darkness. I could barely make out the concrete floor, and the jagged edge where it gave way to the mine. My hand tightened on the doorknob.

I wonder how far down it goes.

In all the commotion from earlier, we didn't get much time to really inspect the damage. The fireman kept us far away from the basement opening, telling us how dangerous it was. How it only took one wrong step...

I rummaged in my pocket and found a bobby pin. I held my breath, and threw it in. *One-one-thousand... two-one-thousand...*

Three seconds passed before I heard the light *tink* of it hitting rock.

My physics is rusty, but I don't think that mine is only twelve feet deep, like the officer told us.

My heart pounded faster. I pulled out my phone and

turned on the flashlight. The light didn't reach the bottom. Just some wet, glistening rock near the top of the hole. I could see one of our plastic storage bins, spilling out childhood drawings and stuffed animals into the hole. The breeze blew up from the basement, softly fluttering through my hair.

"Echo," I called down.

My blood ran cold.

I dropped the rings. *Clink, clink, clink* as they bounced down the steps. They settled at the bottom of the stairs. For a moment, I hesitated. Then I grabbed the door and slammed it shut.

Because—I swear—mixed in with the overlapping echoes of my own voice, there was a *second* voice. Something that I could tell, on a primal level, *did not belong to me.*

I ran out of the house and back to Gertrude's. Locked the door and snuggled in bed. Roger was already asleep, and I didn't want to tell him about it anyway. He'd just think I'm crazy. *You know he doesn't believe in any kind of paranormal stuff. No way there's just some random person hiding down in our sinkhole.*

Right?

It was around 6 that Roger and I made it back to the house. I thought maybe I could retrieve the rings with magnets, but a quick Google search told me white gold won't stick to magnets.

So I came with a rope.

I tied it tightly around my waist at the top of the stairs. "Don't let go," I said, handing Roger the other end.

"Are you sure you don't want me to go down instead?"

"Oh, *now* you want to help."

He frowned at me.

"If you fall, I won't be able to pull you back up," I said, flicking the light switch. Still dead. I grabbed the flashlight from the floor and clicked it on instead.

That's something I forgot to mention before. When the collapse first happened, the lights were working in the basement... but a few hours later, they didn't. I guess the cave-in damaged the electrical lines or something.

Roger grabbed the other end of the rope, and I started down the stairs, holding the banister in one hand and a flashlight in the other.

I could still feel the draft. A breeze of cool air, rising up from the cavern. The wood creaked underneath me with each step. I tried not to look at the hole. Tried to keep my eyes on the rings.

But I couldn't stop myself.

I looked.

The concrete around the edge was shattered and cracked like glass. Rock and dirt cascaded deeper into the mine. The slow, steady *drip drip drip* of water echoed from deep below. The box of my childhood stuff still teetered on the edge, spilling papers and toys into the hole. A pink teddy bear sat on a rocky ledge just a few feet from the rim.

I swallowed.

Almost 150 feet deep. According to the physics, based on how long it took to hear something fall to the bottom. 15 stories—taller than the building I work in. I could imagine the hole, tunneling deep into the earth, filled with pale eyeless creatures that evolved to live in the darkness.

I took another careful step. And then another. Then I was standing on the last step. I slowly bent down to pick up the rings. My fingers were inches away—

Scrrrtch

A scratching sound from inside the hole.

I swiveled the flashlight to the opening. No movement. *Probably just a mouse or something.* I reached down and picked up the rings. And before I could drop them again, I put them on my finger.

I turned around and started up the stairs—

The rope went slack.

Thump, thump, thump. Soft sounds above me. I flicked the flashlight up—to see the end of the rope bouncing down the stairs.

Roger let go of the rope?!

I ran up the stairs, fear pounding through me. The wood groaned under my feet. "Roger! I *told* you not to let go! What part of that did you not understand?!"

And as my voice echoed around me, I heard it again. The voice.

But this time, it almost sounded like my own.

It was trying to imitate me.

I forced my legs to pump harder. I finally pushed my way to the top stair and stood there, panting, my entire body drenched in cold sweat. Then I slammed the door shut and pulled the deadbolt—something I'd forgotten to do last night.

The hallway was empty.

"Roger?" I called.

No reply.

I finally untied the rope from my waist and dropped it to the ground. The other end of the rope was still in the basement; it passed underneath the door. I sighed, then cupped my hands around my mouth: "Roger! I got the rings safely, no thanks to you!"

A soft *thump* from upstairs.

He went upstairs?! What would he have done if the basement caved in? Left me to die? Swearing under my breath, I started for the stairs.

Shhliip

I whipped around.

The rope. It was slowly moving across the floor. Through the crack under the basement door.

As if something were pulling it.

I ran to the front door. I had no idea where Roger was—getting stuff from upstairs to bring to Gertrude's?!—but I had to get out of here. "Roger? I don't know where you are, but we got to get out of here!" I called, not expecting him to reply.

But this time, he did.

"I'm up here."

I started to turn around... and then stopped.

There was something off about his voice. I couldn't place exactly what it was, but something maybe about the rhythm of the consonants, the emphasis on each syllable. I paused in the foyer, my hand on the doorknob.

"Can you help me with something?" he called down.

I turned around—

The stairs were wet.

Something shiny and dark was smudged all over the wood. Like something had been dragged upstairs.

I ran. Maybe that makes me a coward, but if something had taken Roger, there was no use in me dying too. I ran out into the front yard and called 911. Within ten minutes the police were here. They barged into the house as I stood outside, holding my breath.

Fifteen minutes later, they finally came out.

"We didn't find your husband inside."

The officer grimaced at me. I stared up at him, trying not to cry. "What about the blood?" I whispered. "Was that... was that his?"

He shook his head. "We didn't see any blood."

"There was blood—on the stairs—"

"There's nothing on the stairs. Take a look for yourself if you want."

I did. I walked inside the house... and the stairs were clean. The rope was gone. The house was quiet and filled with natural light.

"I don't understand," I whispered.

The police told me that I could file a missing person's report if my husband didn't show up soon. They assured me that he probably just went out, probably to try and help get this place fixed up.

But I have a horrible feeling he's never coming back.

THE UNCANNY VALLEY

The scariest thing about the uncanny valley is that there must be an evolutionary reason for it. That at some point in time, it was advantageous to be afraid of something that looked human... but wasn't.

—

It all started three weeks ago.

I'm an assistant professor of anthropology at a small university. Specifically, I'm a paleoanthropologist, studying old bones and human evolution. Generally, my work is pretty boring: teaching unappreciative undergrads, doing research on my computer, writing really long papers. It only gets exciting when a field investigator brings back something for us to study.

And that's when the trouble began.

Kevin Chu came in one morning with a huge grin on his face. He and his team had just returned from

England, where they'd been excavating near a Neolithic burial site (Aveline's Hole.) And he'd found something.

Something big.

My heart was pounding in my chest as I walked down the hallway of the storage facility. He'd been so cryptic, calling the entire department in for an emergency meeting. But as I swung the door open, I saw why.

On the table sat a reassembled human skeleton.

A nearly *perfect* one.

"Oh, my God," I gasped.

"She's a beaut, isn't she?" Dr. Katz whispered to me. "Ten thousand years old, female, nearly complete."

He was right. The skull, the ribcage, the curved bones of the arms and legs—they were all there. Only her left femur and a few toe bones seemed to be missing.

"We're going to be famous," I whispered.

Our department had been steadily declining for years. I'd always assumed my job had an expiration date. But now... as I listened to Kevin ramble on about how they found her, I couldn't stop grinning.

But then my smile faded.

There was something... *off*... about the skeleton.

Something that I couldn't quite put my finger on.

I studied the gaping holes where her eyes once were. Her crooked jaw, half-filled with teeth. The long, slender, curved bones that made up her arms and legs.

I'd seen hundreds of skeletons before. This was hardly the scariest thing I'd seen. So why did I feel so... afraid? I glanced around at the other professors—but they were all beaming with pride. Clearly, they weren't feeling what I was.

I looked back down at the skeleton—

And froze.

"Kevin," I cut in.

"Yes, Dr. Vasquez?"

"That's not a human skeleton."

His smile faded. "Uh... what do you mean?"

"The interorbital distance." I stepped towards the skeleton and pointed between the eye sockets. "Her eyes are too close together."

"They look fine to me."

"There's no way her face would structurally hold up, with her eyes that close. The nasal bone would fracture, and the lacrimal bones would deform. And it's not just the skull," I continued, gesturing to her forearm. "You can clearly see the radius is *longer* than the humerus. Her forearms were longer than her upper arms, really?"

Kevin stared at me, at a loss for words.

"I'm sorry, but this is obviously a fake."

The room stirred behind me. I felt bad, but me standing up now was better than the school trying to pass off some 13-year-old's Halloween decoration as a paleologic finding. We'd be the laughingstock. I glanced around the room and then stepped back into the crowd, arms crossed.

Kevin's eyes locked on mine.

And then he smiled.

"We already tested it for authenticity. It's real."

I looked down at the skeleton. Looked back at Kevin.

Glanced at the surrounding professors and researchers, whose eyes were all now on me.

I swallowed.

"I don't know what you found," I replied, my voice barely above a whisper. "But there's no way that thing belongs to *Homo sapiens*."

For a few days, everyone in the department was pissed at me. Dr. Katz told me off, telling me I'd ruined Kevin's big day. The field researchers all gave me dirty looks in the hallway. Even the undergrads seemed to somehow sense the energy against me, and gave me snarky answers in class.

But then, late one night, Kevin Chu came to my office.

I didn't even think anyone else was in the building. I was eating takeout in my office, feet up on the desk, listening to Metallica. I had to submit a grant proposal by the morning and, well, frankly I wasn't exactly looking forward to going back to my shitty apartment. Divorce sucks, and it sucks more when your husband is a sharp-as-nails attorney who'll take you to the cleaners without a second thought.

As soon as I saw him my heart sank. *Oh great. He's here to say his piece, yell at me for stealing his big day.* I braced myself for his rant—

But as he got closer, I realized he didn't look so good. His eyes were bloodshot, his hair was greasy, and when he reached the chair on the other side of the desk he collapsed in it panting like he'd just run a mile.

"It's not human," he said, not even looking at me. "Fuck, it's not human, not even in the slightest."

"Uh..."

"You were right. There's something... very wrong... with her. It's not just her eyes, her arms. All her proportions are off. Her legs are longer than they should be. So are her fingers. Her pelvis is wide enough to classify her as female, but it's... well, it's not really the right shape of a normal human pelvis. The iliac crest isn't curved right."

I stared at him, my heart starting to pound.

"So I thought... I thought she might've had a congenital abnormality, you know? Some sort of medical condition that made her proportions different. Even though the irregularities didn't match anything we know of in modern science, maybe there was some ancient syndrome she suffered, or something. But this morning... the DNA analysis came back. And it doesn't match *Homo sapiens*."

I let out a gasp.

"It couldn't be a new human ancestor, could it?" he whispered.

"Not at only 10,000 years old," I said, twirling the same noodle over and over again with my fork. "What did Dr. Katz say?"

He shook his head. "Dr. Katz won't even engage me on this. He went on this whole rant, telling me I didn't know what I was talking about, that I was going to ruin it for everyone. Told me to redo all the tests from the beginning." He finally met my eyes. "And I dunno... I didn't like his tone. Or the others'. It almost feels conspiratorial. Like they don't want me to question things..." He sucked in a breath. "Do you think you can meet me at the lab tomorrow afternoon?"

"Sure."

He pushed out his chair and started to get up. But then he paused, in front of my desk, locking eyes with me. "Maria?"

"Yeah?"

He let out a shuddering breath. "I have to admit, I'm terrified. We have this skeleton, that looks almost human... but *isn't*."

The "uncanny valley"—the fear we feel when we something that looks human, but is just a *little* off—isn't a new concept. It's gained popularity recently with the rise of creepy humanoid robots, but even Sigmund Freud talked about it in 1919, using dolls and wax figures as examples.

He thought our fear came from the idea that if inanimate objects looked like us, maybe they could have a soul. Evolutionary scientists, on the other hand, had a different theory. They said people infected with a communicable disease will look and act a little *off*—so, if that instinctually scared us, it would help us survive.

But this skeleton wasn't a human with some communicable disease. Unless that disease involved reshaping bone and altering DNA.

I stared down at the remains on the table. Trying to imagine what a human woman with this skeleton would look like. But the only images that popped into my head looked like they came out of a horror movie—creepy women with eyes too close together, arms too long, long hair falling over their faces as they stared at me with white, blank eyes.

"The stress marks on the scaphoid suggest torsional load-bearing," Kevin said, circling around the table to join me. "I think she spent a good amount of time on all fours."

"... What?"

He pointed at the small marks on the wrist bones. There was a rushing sound in my ears, as I stared down at the yellowed bone. "That's... horrifying," I finally muttered.

"What about this *isn't* horrifying?" he replied. "Why couldn't I have found some fucking pottery or something instead?"

I finally tore my eyes away from her. "Did you find anything else around her? Any evidence of other humans settling there?"

"Well, *I* didn't. But her skeleton was found only five miles from Aveline's Hole. You know, the burial site, near where they found the Cheddar Man—"

"Right. So she... could be connected to them, in some way. Could've interacted with them."

"Could've."

I stared down at the yellowed skull. The dark, lifeless holes where her eyes would've been. That were just a bit too close together. The eternal smile of her crooked teeth, with her mandible too large for the rest of her skull.

And then I saw it.

"Uh... Kevin?"

Kevin came around to stand next to me. I pointed at the side of her skull, trying to find the words. My throat was dry. "She... she doesn't have a coronal suture. Or any of the other sutures. Her skull... it's all one bone."

"What?"

We stared in horror at the skull. My mind was racing a thousand miles a minute—I knew what it must mean, but it didn't make sense. There was no way. Was there?

I sucked in a shaky breath. "Without them, her skull wouldn't be able to mold during birth. Or grow, as she grew."

Kevin's face dropped. "You mean..."

"Her skull has been the same size her entire life." I stared at the skeleton beneath me, spots of darkness starting to shimmer at the edge of my vision. "She was never born. She was never a child. She just... came into being... like this."

I found that our discovery wasn't the only one of its kind.

In the past 50 years, three other skeletons had been found similar to ours. Absence of skull sutures; strange stress marks that implied walking on all fours; physiological anomalies that didn't match up with *Homo sapi-*

ens. They ranged from 10,000 years old to, terrifyingly, only 500 years old.

But there was something even stranger about each of the discoveries.

They all seemed to be part of a cover-up.

When the skeletons were retested, the articles claimed, everything matched up. They simply seemed to have deformities that were a result of a genetic disorder. The DNA was human, the skull sutures were there after all, and everything was okay.

The idea that these things *weren't* human was relegated to fringe conspiracy theorists and tabloid papers like *The Sun*.

"Maybe it *is* a human ancestor," Kevin told me, when I shared my research with him.

"That one skeleton was only found 500 years ago, though," I replied. "I think there'd be more of them around if that were true. Or at least, evidence of them in writing, art…"

"Maybe it was a tiny, isolated population."

"The skeletons were found all over, though. Europe, Canada, Brazil."

"Yeah." He shook his head. "I don't know what to make of it."

I stared at the computer screen, unsure what to say. None of this made sense. At all. And I knew one thing: I didn't really want to be in the same room as that skeleton again.

Ever.

"Kevin. Call me back. *Now.*"

"Dammit, Kevin! Pick up the fucking phone!"

"*KEVIN!*"

Kevin wasn't picking up. I sounded halfway deranged in my voicemails, but I had good reason to be. Because after staying up all night... I'd found something.

Something so horrible that it made my blood turn to ice.

I found a post on a forum. Then I made a series of calls: to a hospital, to a morgue, to a police station. And after pulling at all the threads, there was one man willing to talk to me: a gruff, old detective by the name of Jack Thomas.

After a six-hour car ride, I was there.

"The morgue called me about a Jane Doe," he said, as he leaned back in his moldy-green recliner. His living room looked like a time capsule: wood-paneled walls, orange carpet, a record player in the corner. The man in front of me looked close to 80, with steel-gray curly hair that contrasted sharply with his brown skin. But his mind was sharp as a tack.

"This was two days after New Year's Eve. 1983. The Jane Doe was found up on the mountain, off one of the hiking trails. We thought she was some partier, maybe, that had gotten drunk and wandered off and died. There wasn't any obvious sign of foul play. We couldn't identify her by her dental records, or anything else. She had no tattoos, no birthmarks, nothing like that.

"And that wasn't unusual. But then... the coroner...

he pulled me aside. *There's something wrong with that woman,* he told me. And the coroner, he was a skeptical kind of guy, not religious or into the supernatural or anything like that. Not afraid to poke around dead bodies all day, either. So to see him scared... it was something else.

"*Her arms are too long,* he told me. *All her proportions are off.* And when he brought me in to take a look at the body, I saw he was right. There was something terribly *off* about that woman. It haunts me to this day. Her eyes..." He trailed off, shaking his head.

All the blood drained from my face.

This wasn't some ancient woman. Some ancient creature. There was something existing with us, evolving with us, living on the outskirts of society. Haunting us. And we'd found evidence, we'd found bodies.

And every single time, it was covered up.

"Kevin, dammit, I'm driving to your house," I said in my final voicemail, before I got in the car and drove to his place.

Kevin is gone.

I went to his house. His wife doesn't know where he is. She's in the process of filing a missing persons report. He's still not picking up his phone.

And I have a horrible feeling he never will.

The evidence for this... thing has been covered up, swept under the rug, for decades. Centuries. Someone wants this thing to survive. To continue stalking us. Evolving with us. With how long the secret has been kept, I'm sure many have died in their struggle for the truth.

And I fear that I may be next.

I've been driving for two days now. Soon I'll be starting my life over, taking on a new name, cutting off my old life. But I will continue searching for the truth.

I'm moving into a house that borders thousands of acres of deep woods. Maybe, if I'm lucky, one day I'll look out my window—

And see a woman standing there, with eyes too close and arms too long, staring back at me.

MY ROOMMATE IS TRYING TO KILL ME

It's no secret that my roommate and I don't like each other.

I found her a few months ago after my other roommate dropped out of school. I didn't vet her much, because I needed to find someone *fast* to cover half the rent. Of course I did a background check, stalked her social media, that kind of thing. But I'd only actually talked to her one-on-one for twenty minutes before she moved in.

She's mid-twenties like me, and very pretty. Perfect blonde hair and clear blue eyes. Perfectly applied makeup, from pink eyeshadow to skin that looked like it had been airbrushed on. Sparkly white teeth with a killer smile.

I think that's why I didn't spend more time vetting her. I assumed she must be okay because she *looks* okay.

I immediately regretted my decision.

Apparently, Emily is a "beauty vlogger." She doesn't

have a real job—just sits in her room all day, trying out different makeup looks for her fans. I hear her up at all hours of the night, even, talking and giggling as she records.

But at least she pays her rent. So I didn't grumble as I cleaned up the foundation powder from our counter (seriously, what does this woman's skin really look like? She applies like a metric ton of foundation to her face every day.) I didn't complain when she woke me up at 2 AM with a fit of high-pitched giggles—or when I had to leave the windows open in freezing cold just to get rid of that horrible floral scent. She tried to befriend me at first, but after I sniped at her a few times, she got the message. We pleasantly ignored each other, as if an unspoken pact had been made. Things were actually fine.

That all changed on September 7th.

I was running late. I didn't let the shower water run for a few minutes like I usually do. I jumped right in—and as soon as my feet hit the ceramic, they slipped out from under me.

If I hadn't grabbed the curtain rod just in time, I would've cracked my head open.

"I'm so sorry. I'm trying out this new conditioner," Emily explained, when I told her. "It's super detangling. I never really noticed but I guess the bathtub does get kind of slippery. I'm so sorry."

She was being really nice about it, but I was furious. It was bad enough that she messed up the place with all her beauty gook. Now, it was a safety hazard, too?

"I can't keep doing this," I said, trying to keep my

voice from rising. "You have to keep all your makeup in your bedroom. I'm sick of cleaning up all your messes. And you can't use weird shit in the shower that might kill me. Okay?"

"Okay," she said in a small voice.

Emily was really good about keeping her stuff out of the bathroom after that. The bathtub was never slippery, and I even noticed that cloying floral scent seemed to fade. I was happy, and even felt a little bad for yelling at her so much. She pays half the rent just like I do. Why do I get to say what comes into the bathroom and what doesn't?

But then it got worse.

On September 30th, I woke up early. Made my way to the fridge and, shamelessly, grabbed the milk to take a swig right out of the carton. Emily drinks fat-free, so the 2% is all mine.

But as soon as the milk hit my tongue, I began to sputter.

"Eugh! What—what *is* this?!"

The milk didn't taste just sour. It was acrid, burning my tongue and making my eyes tear.

I ran over to the sink and spit it out. It had a strange consistency—like it had been diluted with something clear and slightly viscous. Like spit or something.

Emily burst out of her bedroom. "What happened?"

"Something is *really* wrong with this milk."

"Oh my God, you drank the milk?"

A funny feeling settled in my stomach. "Why... why would I *not* drink the milk?"

"I told you! Last night! I asked you if I could use your

milk carton for a beauty mask recipe. You said sure. So I poured the remaining milk into a cup--" she pointed to an aluminum-foil-covered mug in the fridge-- "and used the carton for the mask."

I cupped my hands under the faucet. Swished water in my mouth. Over and over until the acrid taste started to fade. She kept apologizing, but I could barely hear her voice over the faucet.

That night I couldn't sleep.

I don't remember her asking me about the milk carton. That thought pulsed in my brain well into the wee hours. I got up, turned the lock, and jimmied a chair underneath the doorknob for good measure.

And why my milk carton? She could've used a bowl, a bottle, a Ziploc bag. And I don't know what the hell she put in her beauty mask, but it sure tasted like poison.

I kept even more distance from Emily for the next few days, trying to figure out what to do. Kicking her out would most likely result in me having to move, too, unless I could find someone else to take her place within a matter of days. *And I'm probably just being paranoid.* She was a beauty vlogger, and making some weird-ass face mask sounds just like the kind of thing that would go viral.

That's what I told myself--until Friday happened.

I got home late that night, a little drunk. I unlocked the door, yawning, and stepped inside. Then I flicked the light switch.

It didn't go on.

Dammit. The bulb must've blown. The light was on

in the main hallway, so it couldn't be a power outage. Still—the apartment was pitch dark. I fumbled through the darkness, my footsteps weaving from the alcohol, my hands stretched out in front of me--

They met something soft.

What is that?

I was standing in the middle of the main room. There was only the couch and TV in there. It should've been a clear shot to my bedroom door.

I squinted into the darkness. Nothing. But it was weird—I could tell something was there. By the way the hum of the fridge muffled right in front of me. How the slight variations in black and gray changed just two feet in front of my face.

This is stupid. I reached into my pocket, pulled out my phone, and hit the flashlight.

My heart dropped.

Emily stood right in front of me.

Just standing there in the middle of the room. At almost 2 AM. She faced away from me, towards the windows. Her blonde hair cascaded down her back, glinting off the phone's flashlight.

"E-emily?" I backed away. "What are you doing up so late?"

She slowly turned around.

She was grinning.

A wide, ear-to-ear grin. Her blue eyes sparkled in the light as she stared at me.

And then she giggled.

A low giggle in her throat. As if she were positively delighted that I'd just arrived home. It made her entire body shake—and that's when I noticed something glinting in her hand.

A knife.

I forced my legs to move. Forced myself to run towards the apartment door. But as soon as I took a step, I heard her lunge after me. Her fingers grabbed my hair—*tug*—and then I jerked forward with all my strength, ripping several out in the process.

I made it to the door and burst into the hallway. Ran down the stairs, screaming the entire time. Someone must've dialed 911 because minutes after I made it to the parking lot, red and blue lights were throbbing in the darkness, sirens wailing in my ears.

The police found Emily in the apartment. They arrested her and told me later that "Emily Ryan" was a fake name; though they haven't been able to identify her yet. However, she did admit one thing that chilled me to the bone.

Emily never had a beauty vlog.

I ACCIDENTALLY SUMMONED STAN INSTEAD OF SATAN

We found the plans online.

My best friend Lilith and I have always been interested in the macabre. (Ok, her real name isn't Lilith, it's Katie. But I call her Lilith.) Our parents think we're "goth," but we're not. Those are the kids that wear too much eyeliner and write cringey depressed poems. We do cooler stuff, like hold seances and read dark magic spellbooks and obsess over the Salem witches.

So when Lilith found plans online to summon Satan, I was SO excited.

"Are we seriously going to try to summon *Satan?!*" I whispered, my heart pounding in my chest.

"Why not?" Lilith answered, as she pulled out her phone and brought up the plans. "It's easy. We just have to draw this giant pentagram on the floor... and say this stuff in French..."

"That's *Latin*," I corrected.

"Latin. What*ever*. Nerd." She rolled her eyes at me.

"And then we write 'SATAN' in blood in the middle of the pentagram."

"That sounds too easy," I said, frowning. "If it was that easy, wouldn't everyone summon Satan like all the time?"

"You think normies want to summon Satan?"

"No..."

She unzipped her bag and pulled out a black Sharpie. "Then let's get to work."

It was hard work. My room has a really fluffy carpet, so I had to draw each stroke several times over before it was actually visible. "Are you sure this comes out with soap? My mom will *kill* me."

"Shut up and keep drawing," she replied, furiously scribbling with the marker.

After twenty minutes or so, we were finally done. I stood up and admired our handiwork: a pentagram in a circle, with several strange symbols inside each cavity of the pentagram. It looked good. Part of me hoped it wouldn't wash out—how mad would Mom be if I had a literal SATAN SUMMONING CIRCLE on my bedroom floor?

Ooooh. That would *really* get her goat. And she totally deserved it, after not letting me go to Sadie's sleepover. I swear, sometimes I was so mad at her I wanted her to die.

"Okay. Now the Latin stuff." Lilith pulled out her phone and began to read. "*Ego te voco...*" She read the entire thing, terribly. I mean I don't know Latin but listening to it was painful.

"Now the blood," I said, scowling. "Wait. Did you

bring blood?"

She tapped her arm. "We use our own blood, silly."

"Like we actually have to cut ourselves?"

She nodded.

"I dunno, Lil. That sounds kind of... extreme."

"Don't be such a baby," she said. And then, before I could stop her, she grabbed my hand and knicked my palm with the scissors she'd been hiding in her sleeve.

"LILITH!" I shouted. "What the *hell* are you doing?!"

"Stop wasting time. We gotta do it before the blood dries up." She reached out for my hand. "Here. You write the first three letters and I'll write the last two. Saves time."

I was mad, but she was right. We were running out of time.

We bent over the carpet and got to work.

Writing stuff in blood is totally overrated. They make it sound like this cool soulbinding thing but it actually sucks. My hand was stinging and writing just that first letter, *S*, was enough that I needed a break. *Why didn't we use Lilith's blood?!* I thought as I closed my eyes, breathing hard, trying not to focus on the pain. Then I sucked in a breath and got back to work, sticking my finger against my palm and writing the *T*.

Breathless, we both got up and stepped away from the circle.

And that's when we saw it.

"You *idiot!*" Lilith said. "You forgot the *A!*"

She was right. The letters in blood read *STAN*.

"Oh no. Uh, I'll fix it." I looked down at the wound

on my hand—but it'd stopped bleeding. "It's dried up. Get the scissors and cut your hand—"

"I'm not cutting my hand!"

"Are you serious?! You literally STABBED me!"

"Just squeeze your hand and more blood will come out."

"I don't want to! It—"

We were both cut off by a low humming sound.

We both turned to the circle, our hearts pounding.

"Holy shit," I whispered, as the Sharpie-engraved pentagram began to glow. Dim red light that pulsed like a heartbeat; then faster and faster, brighter and brighter, as a horrible roar rushed in our ears—

POP.

We both stared, mouths agape.

There was not a demon in the center of the circle. Not a leather-skinned, fiery-eyed, red-horned creature from the depths of hell.

No... there was just a guy.

An average-looking white guy. Maybe in his twenties or early thirties. He was wearing a gray T-shirt and khaki-colored cargo pants. There was stubble on his jaw and his hair was kind of messy.

"You called me?" he asked.

Lilith and I stared at each other. I made an unintelligible stuttering noise.

"I'm Stan," he said. Then he let out a yawn that exposed his yellowed, crooked teeth. "You need help or something?"

"How—how did you get in here?" I finally asked, composing myself.

"You summoned me."

"Um," Lilith interjected. "We were TRYING to summon SATAN."

"Oh. Common mistake. That pesky little extra 'A', huh?"

I backed away, still staring in horror at this man who had just popped out of thin air. I wanted to believe that this guy had somehow broken in. Maybe climbed in through a window while I wasn't looking. But the truth is, I *was* looking. And I saw him just *appear,* right there, in the middle of the circle.

Lilith and I never should've gotten involved in this stuff, I thought. I felt like I was going to throw up. *It was fun to talk about demons and dark magic and Salem witches... when, deep down, I didn't ACTUALLY believe any of it. But now... I just saw a man pop out of thin air. Just like that.*

"Maybe... maybe I should call my parents," I stuttered to Lilith.

"You'll be grounded forever."

That was true. I *would* be grounded forever. Maybe we could just... get rid of him somehow. "Hey, um, my mom has some really expensive jewelry in her room. Why don't you just take that... and leave?"

"I don't really need the money," he replied in his nasally voice. "But thanks anyway."

"Um. Well, you can't stay here."

"I like your room," he said, ignoring my comment. "Is that a Black Sabbath CD? Your parents let you listen to that? What are you, like, 14?"

"Uh..."

"I mean, that's cool to have permissive parents,"

Stan said, shrugging. "I guess I should've guessed that, since they let you draw a pentagram on the floor and all."

"They're not permissive," I replied quietly.

"You're just good at hiding stuff then, yeah?"

He stepped out of the pentagram and started towards my desk. Picked up the Black Sabbath CD, then pulled out a drawer and rummaged through some of the contents. "Mmm. These are awesome," he said, holding up one of my Milky Pens. "Love these things. You probably got 'em 'cause they draw on black paper, right? So you can have a whole, like, goth journal?"

Lilith and I stared at him, speechless.

"We're not goth," Lilith finally whispered.

"Yeah, yeah, emo or something though right?" He let out a laugh. "You gotta be *something* to try and summon Satan."

Lilith turned to me as he bent over the other desk drawer. "We've got to get him out of here. He's probably dangerous. And if your parents see him..."

I nodded. Slowly, I took a step towards him, standing as straight as I possibly could. "Listen. I'm sorry Stan, but you have to leave. My dad has a rifle and he'll shoot you as soon as he gets back—"

Lilith jabbed me in the ribs. "*Don't—tell—him—we're—home—alone,*" she whispered through gritted teeth.

"—And my older brother is napping in the basement. He's going to come up and beat the crap out of you. So you better go."

Stan finally stopped rummaging in the drawer.

Slowly, he turned around. Straightened up before me. Then his mouth stretched into a grin that showed off his yellow teeth.

"But you don't have a brother, Ava."

My heart dropped. I looked at Lilith—she looked back at me. And then as if communicating by telepathy, we both raced for the door at the same time.

Surprisingly he didn't follow us as we raced down the stairs. Panting, I grabbed Lilith's hand and dragged her towards the kitchen, towards the sliding glass door. We could run right to the Thompson's on the other side, tell them someone had broken in—

I skidded to a stop.

The refrigerator door hung open. And underneath the crack, I spotted his dirty white sneakers.

"Going so soon?" Stan asked, as he swung the door closed. "Hey, do you have anything good to eat around here? Maybe those little, like, puffed cheese things with the cheetah on the bag?"

We backed away.

"Hey. Listen now. You two are the ones who summoned *me*," he said. "You're not going to just kick me out, are you?"

"Will you go if I give you Cheetos?" I asked in a small voice.

He shrugged. "Maybe. Why, you have any?"

I ducked into the pantry, grabbed the orange bag, and blindly threw it at him. "Here! Now *get out!*"

"Now wait a second," he said, plopping down on a chair, propping his feet up on the kitchen table. He opened the bag with a loud *POP*. "If you were summoning Satan, you were clearly trying to make a deal with him. Right?" He threw some Cheetos in his mouth and crunched on them loudly. "I want that same deal."

"We were just summoning Satan for fun—"

"Yeah, right." *Crunch, crunch.* "So what was the deal going to be? What did you want?"

Lilith and I glanced at each other.

For a long moment, there was silence. Stan staring expectantly at both of us; Lilith and I glancing nervously at each other. Finally, I sucked in a shuddering breath.

"Please. Go," I choked out.

"Alrighty then." He held up his cheese-covered hands in surrender. "Y'know, I was just trying to be polite. Offer my services. Make sure you got something out of that whole summoning business. But I'll go. Plain and simple."

And with that, he got up and walked out of the kitchen. A second later, I heard the door swing open and slam shut.

Lilith and I stared at each other in silence.

We only moved when the shrill ring of the telephone jolted through the silence. I glanced over—no one ever called the home phone anymore. We only kept it around for my dad's long business calls, really. But it was nine o'clock—too late for that.

I stepped towards the phone, confused, and slowly picked it up. "Hello?" I asked in a soft voice.

"Ava?" The voice on the other end of the line was shaking, but I recognized it immediately. It was my sister, Sam.

"Sam?"

"I'm so sorry," she said, through breaking sobs. "But they just... they just told me... it's Mom and Dad." She sucked in a breath. "They got in a terrible accident on Route 40. Dad's being airlifted to the hospital but Mom... Mom..."

My heart sunk.

"She's dead, Ava."

The phone fell from my hands and clattered on the floor.

But all I could picture in my head was Stan. With his yellowed grin and steel-gray eyes.

Smugly smiling at providing his 'services.'

I SEE PEOPLE HIDING THEIR FACES

I first noticed it in a photo from Kasey's birthday party. There was a group photo of us, all huddled together, smiling for the camera. But between me and Jack, you could see a man sitting at a table behind us. He was hiding his face in his hands.

"Guess that guy doesn't like to be photographed," Jack laughed.

"Yeah."

"Makes sense though. Who wants strangers having a picture of you, you know? Especially with all the weird facial recognition and stuff cameras do nowadays?"

It was still weird, though. Looking at the picture sent chills down my spine. I mean, his face was turned directly towards the camera. If he really didn't want to be photographed, couldn't he have just tilted his head way down or put the menu in front of it?

Why the creepy "weeping angels" pose?

But some people are weird about being

photographed. My brother never smiles for family photos, just to annoy my mom. One of my college friends has to have like five pounds of makeup on her face before she's willing to be in a photo.

Maybe this guy always hid his face in his hands like that. He thought he was being funny or something.

And so I forgot about it.

A few days later, though...

I went to the grocery store after work. I passed a little girl in the bread aisle, standing next to her mom. As I passed, I looked down to give her a little wave— And stopped dead.

She was hiding her face in her hands.

Just like the guy in the photograph. *Relax, she's probably just crying about something,* I told myself, as I hurried away.

But then why was her face turning in time with mine?

As though she were watching me, between the cracks in her fingers?

I threw my groceries on the conveyor belt. The cashier raised her eyebrow as the carton of eggs fell with a loud rattling sound.

"Um—"

"I'm in a hurry," I breathed as I ran over to the keypad and stuck my card in.

It had started to rain. Light, pattering raindrops fell on the windshield, bleeding into little rivers that distorted the road before me. *Swish*—I turned on the wipers and they swept through.

I couldn't stop my fingers from frenetically tapping the wheel.

You have to calm down.

Don't let this be like last time.

I rushed into the house, the rain a downpour now. By the time I got inside, my shirt was damp, sticking to my skin.

"Jenny? You're back earl—"

I raced up the stairs and ran into the bathroom. My hands shook as I grabbed a pill bottle out of the medicine cabinet. The pills rattled loudly inside, like a warning sign. And the letters printed across it read *EXP 04/21.*

But I couldn't. I just couldn't.

"Jenny?" Jack called through the door. "Are you okay?"

"I'm fine. Just... have a bad headache."

I spent the rest of the evening wrapped up in a blanket, watching some stupid Hallmark movie, as Jack listened to some podcast downstairs. And now--I don't know if it was time, or the meds--I almost laughed at the incident earlier.

I almost had a panic attack because some little girl was crying at the store?

So stupid.

God forbid someday I'll actually have real problems, real things to panic about.

I fell into a peaceful, dreamless sleep. The next morning I went to work as usual. That was a good sign--last time I'd had a panic attack, I'd had to call in sick.

I took the elevator up to the fifth floor, humming to

myself. Sat down in my office and worked on emails for an hour over coffee.

And then it happened.

Taking a little break, I walked over to the window. I looked down at all the people, hurrying along on the sidewalks down below--

But one was standing still.

A woman. In a black dress. Looking straight up at me.

But of course, she wasn't *actually* looking. Because her hands were hiding her face. In that same, creepy, peekaboo pose that the other two had.

The blood drained out of my face.

What. The. Fuck.

I backed away from the window. Kept backing away until my leg collided with my desk. I yelped as I fell backwards, grabbing the edge of the desk just at the last second.

Breathing hard, I collapsed into the chair.

I left work early, claiming I felt sick, and got into bed for the rest of the day. I kept telling myself that I shouldn't freak out, and there were perfectly good reasons for what I'd seen.

Coincidence.

Flash mob.

Weird conspiracy plot by my ex-boyfriend to scare me.

The doorbell ringing snapped me out of my thoughts. Jack was still at work so I went downstairs. My hand fell on the doorknob, and I was about to open it... but something in me made me pause. A sort of itchy, tingly feeling, like I was being watched.

I lifted my face and brought my eye to the peephole.
No.
There on the front porch stood our elderly neighbor, Mrs. Rose. Except—her face was hidden in her hands. Just like all the other people I'd seen. That creepy, peek-aboo pose, wrinkled spotted hands covering her face.

I drew the deadbolt and ran upstairs.

But I couldn't just wait for Jack to come home. What if he was hiding his face from me like all the others?

So I called him at work. *Videocalled* him.

I breathed a sigh of relief when he picked up. He wasn't hiding his face. "Hi, love!" he said with a grin. "Videocalling me, huh? What's the occasion?"

"When will you be back?"

His smile faded. "Is something wrong?"

"Everything's fine. Just trying to figure out what to do for din--"

Ding-dong.

The doorbell rang again, echoing up the stairs.

"Is someone at the door?" Jack asked, frowning.

"Yeah, uh, it's just--just a delivery. I'll go get it lat--"

Ding-dong.

"I'll see you soon, bye." Before he could say more, I hung up.

I lay there on the bed, staring up at the ceiling, my heart going a million miles an hour. The doorbell rang once, twice, three more times before it finally stopped.

Thoughts swirled in my head but for some reason, my mind kept boomeranging back to what Dr. Thompson had said, all those years ago.

They aren't following you. He'd leaned towards me in

his seat, dark eyes filled with compassion. *I know... I know that your ex-boyfriend threatened you. But it's been several years. Most likely, if he was going to do something, he would've done it by now.*

I'm going to prescribe you something to help with panic attacks. You're lucky you only hit the curb—you could get into a much more dangerous accident next time...

I was interrupted from my thoughts by the groan of the garage door opening.

I ran down the stairs, my heart racing. The familiar *thump!* of the garage door closing, then the *swush* of the fridge opening. I ran into the kitchen—

And stopped in my tracks.

The fridge door hung open, hiding Jack from view. All I could see were his brown leather shoes, sticking out from under the crack.

"... Jack?"

He didn't reply.

"Jack!"

His foot took a step back. The side of his face slowly came into view around the side of the door. A tuft of dark hair, then an ear—

"Sowwee," he said, gesturing to his full mouth. "I'm starbing."

I collapsed into the kitchen chair. "Oh my God. You scared me."

The fridge door shut. He swallowed. "Sorry. How was your day?"

"Fine. Just fine." I forced a smile. "How was yours?"

He shrugged. "Okay."

I didn't tell him about what I'd seen. But I had to ask

—I had to know. "Hey, Jack, can I ask you something?" I got out my phone and pulled up the photo from Kasey's birthday party. "That guy in the background. What is he doing?"

"Uh... we already talked about this yesterday. He's hiding his face from the camera because he doesn't want to be photographed or whatever."

"Yes, but *how*? What exactly is he doing?"

Jack gave me a weird look. "He's doing this," he said. He raised his hands to his face, in the same peekaboo pose.

Fear shot through me. I grabbed his arms and pulled them away from his face. "Don't *do* it!"

"Okay?" he said, uncertainly.

"Sorry. I just... nevermind." I put away my phone and stood up. "I'm going to cook some pasta, I think. Want me to put on extra for you?"

"Sure."

So I'm not imagining it, I thought, as I poured water into the pot. *It's not some weird hallucination or something. There is photographic evidence that at least one guy was hiding his face like that.* At that moment, I wanted to tell Jack everything. But I couldn't. Jack would no doubt just sigh and set up another appointment with Dr. Thompson.

I loved Jack, but that was the one thing I hated about him. Opening up to him often meant suggestions of appointments, or vacations, or books to read. Not just... engaging with me and trying to help me work through it.

The rest of the evening went okay, though. Mrs.

Rose didn't come to the door anymore, and Jack and I even had a nice dinner together. I eventually fell into a deep sleep, comforted by the sound of Jack breathing next to me.

I woke with a start.

The bedroom was dark. Shafts of moonlight fell through the curtains, falling on the soft bedding. I sucked in a breath and rolled over, reaching for Jack. But as my arm wrapped around his waist, I noticed something odd.

His arms weren't splayed out straight in front of him, like they usually were. Instead, the elbows were bent...

My heart dropped.

"Jack?" I whispered.

He was still as a statue. Facing away from me. His chest slightly rising and falling with each breath.

"Jack!" I said, louder this time.

And then he did it. He rolled towards me, slowly.

My blood turned to ice.

He was hiding his face.

His hands were pressed against his face in that horrible weeping angels pose. He didn't say anything—didn't move—just lay there, facing me.

This close up, I realized—the slivers of darkness between his fingers. There was something horribly wrong with them. They looked too dark, even in the darkness of the bedroom. I couldn't see the glint of his eyes, or any details of his face. Just... a black void.

I screamed.

His face slowly tilted up as I jumped out of the bed. As if he could see me between the cracks of his fingers.

I jumped out of bed and ran into the hallway. I could hear his footsteps behind me, creaking across the old wood. I stumbled down the stairs and ran through the kitchen. His bare feet slapped on the tile behind me. I ran into the garage, panting. Grabbed my keys and dove into my car.

I didn't dare look at him as I peeled out of the driveway.

I drove into town. It was a little after 3 AM—the streets were empty. All the little shops that lined the sidewalk were dark. I drove around Main Street for several minutes, in a loop, without even really realizing what I was doing.

What the hell is going on?

Paranoid delusions. That's what Dr. Thompson had called them. But I never hallucinated anything before. Just thought people were watching me, that the house was bugged, that my ex was stalking me. And I'd moved past that. The worst of it was years ago. I'd moved on, forward, gotten married and started a new life.

Besides. Jack had seen the man hiding his face in the photo. That was proof that I wasn't imagining it.

I pulled over and parked outside of the bookstore. I

made sure my doors were locked and then pulled out my phone. *People hiding their face,* I typed into the search bar—but that just brought up a bunch of silly stock images. *People covering their face with their hands.* Again, more stock images. *People following me hiding their faces like weeping angels in Doctor Who.*

Bingo.

Among all the hits for the Doctor Who wiki was a forum post. Dated a few months ago, by a user named **purplehairedgurl55.**

I keep seeing these people, hiding their faces in their hands. Sort of like the weeping angels in Doctor Who. I see them in random places—on the subway, at the store. It's so weird. Anyone else see this? Is this some sort of like, advertisement or psychological experiment or something?

There were a bunch of replies. Most of them weren't helpful, just people commenting things like "wow," "creepy," "update plz." But one stood out. A warning, in all caps:

DO NOT LET THEM SEE YOUR FACE.

I stared at the phone, my heart sinking. They'd already seen my face—all of them. Did that mean... I scrolled down.

There was one last post from **purplehairedgurl55.**

I just got back from class and MY ROOMMATE WAS DOING IT. I tried talking to her and everything but she wouldn't say anything. Just stared at me with her fucking hands over her fucking face. What the HELL is going on??

And that was it. The last post from her. Not only on the thread, but sitewide.

I swallowed.

Whatever happened to her... is going to happen to me.

My heart pounded in my chest. That horrible, familiar spiral of dread, pulling me down into nothing. I tried to focus on my breathing. *In, out. In, out.* But the weight didn't stop—I was drowning—I couldn't—

Tap-tap-tap.

A soft tapping on the window.

I looked up. *Oh, no.*

Standing right outside my window was a police officer. Behind me, in the rearview mirror, there was a police cruiser parked with its lights off.

"License and registration," came the muffled voice from the window.

I leaned over and opened the glove compartment. Pulled out the license and registration. Breathed in and out, trying to swallow the dizzying panic building in my chest. *You can't have an attack right now. Jack is still your emergency contact and he'll call him if you're ill. Or, worse, drop you off at home to get some rest...*

Normal. Calm. Breathe in. Out.

I turned to the window, rolled it down, and offered the documents.

He didn't react.

He can't be one of them. From this angle, I couldn't see his face, but I could see his hands. They were hanging at his sides—not held up to his face. *I'm okay. It's just some officer asking why you're parked on the road at 3 AM. Which is a totally valid question.*

But he still wasn't taking the documents, either.

"...Officer?"

He bent his head down—

He didn't have a face.

The sides of his head just suddenly ended, into an empty nothingness where his face should have been. Darkness. A void. A pit. The complete absence of anything.

I screamed.

He grabbed the bottom of the window and shoved his head inside. I felt a horrible, invisible pull on my own face. Like a thousand tiny magnets were just underneath the surface of my skin, pulling at my entire face, sucking it into the void—

I reached over and slammed the button to roll up the window.

His fingers gripped the edge of the window. Pushing it down with inhuman strength. The window made a horrible ratcheting whine as it tried to roll up, but couldn't. The man pushed further into the car. His lack-of-face inches from mine.

Hot pain bloomed across my face as the pull grew stronger. I looked into that horrible darkness, the nothingness, and dread flooded through my body.

This is it.

This is how I die.

But then seven words popped into my head.

DO NOT LET THEM SEE YOUR FACE.

I raised my shaking hands. Slowly put them up to my face, blocking the view of that horrible void. The pain seared across my skin but I ignored it.

I pushed my hands against my face.

And just like that. The pain stopped. A silence filled

the car, ringing in my ears. Seconds ticked by—and then I heard footsteps against the pavement.

He was leaving.

I waited until I heard the door of his cruiser slam. Only then did I take my hands away from my face. Then I jabbed the starter button—the engine roared to life—I slammed my foot on the accelerator.

The car peeled out onto the road.

I turned every which way, making sharp turns and taking back roads, until I'd lost the police car. Then I was coasting down the highway, destination nowhere, trying to figure out what to do now.

One thing was certain: I couldn't go home.

I pictured Jack, lying in our bed, with that horrible emptiness instead of the face I loved. Who had stolen his face? Had one of the faceless come to him? Maybe Mrs. Rose rang the doorbell again after I'd fallen asleep. Maybe he'd answered it.

And now he was gone.

MY HUSBAND MAKES ME WEAR A WIG

I knew Mark was a widower when I met him. And honestly, I was relieved. Of course I wasn't happy that somebody died. But at my age (37), most of the men I met on Match.com were divorcees whose wives had left them for good reason. Affairs. Gambling. Really, *really* poor hygiene.

So Mark was a standout. Nothing had gone wrong in his marriage; his wife had just, sadly, gotten cancer and passed away. After a few dates, I knew he was "the one." From his twinkling blue eyes to his infectious smile, from the way he asked about my day to the way he held me on cold nights, he was wonderful.

Of course nobody's perfect though, and that's where the wig comes in.

He brought it out three months after we'd gotten married. "Would you be open to wearing this sometimes?" he asked with a sheepish grin.

I couldn't help but laugh. It was so stereotypical:

bleach-blonde hair, coiffed in a blowout sort of hairstyle, with long curtain bangs that curled at the bottom. I began to giggle. "Um. I guess? You're into that, huh?"

 I wasn't blonde. Far from it—my hair was nearly black, from my Hispanic ancestry on my dad's side. But it didn't bother me. If I were younger I'd be up all night, wondering if he secretly hated how I looked. But now I was old enough to know people have fantasies. Hell, maybe I'd ask him to apply a temporary tattoo to his bicep, next time.

 "You want me to wear it tonight?" I asked in a sultry voice.

 "Maybe."

 "Mm. Sounds fun." I reached out to touch the wig—

 He took a sudden step back. So that it was just out of my reach. "Sorry," he said hastily. "This is just, a really expensive wig. The oil on your hands... over time, it'll damage it."

 That annoyed me. Here I was, being super open to whatever fantasy he was going to throw at me, and he was mad that I'd *damage* it. But whatever. "Sorry. Won't touch it."

 "So tonight then?" he asked, with a big stupid grin on his face.

 "Tonight."

He waited in the bedroom while I put the wig on.

 I'd only worn a wig once before. When I was a

teenager, dressing up as Morticia Addams. It was one of those cheap, plasticky ones from Party City.

But this one... Mark wasn't kidding, it must've been expensive. The blonde hair, besides being perfectly coiffed, had a natural sheen that was neither too shiny nor too dull. Even though it was a cheap bleach-blonde color, there was beautiful variation in the strands. Bright flaxen highlights on top of gold and taupe.

The only part that seemed "cheap" was the cap, or scalp, or whatever you call the thing that the hair attaches to. It was stiff and rough under my fingers, and an ugly mottled tan color. I wasn't sure how exactly I was supposed to get it attached to my head. Maybe bobby pins?

"You almost ready?" Mark called from the bedroom.

"Yeah! Just a minute."

I brought the wig up to my face, careful to touch the hair as little as possible. As soon as I did, I wrinkled my nose. It smelled overly flowery. Like someone had doused it in perfume. Where had Mark been storing this thing?

After several minutes and twenty bobby pins, I got it on.

I hope this doesn't take long.

Damn, I know that's a horrible thing to think before having sex. But I didn't like the way it felt on my head. It felt oddly heavy, pulling at my scalp every time I moved. And it was weird having hair brushing my shoulders that *wasn't mine.*

"Okay," I called out. "I'm ready."

We made love, and it was incredible. The kind of earth-shattering experience that makes you feel like you left your body, maybe this entire world, for a moment.

It bothered me a little, actually. Why wasn't our sex this good when I *wasn't* wearing the wig? Maybe he really *was* into blondes? I found myself researching Schwarzenkopf bleach on my coffee break. Even though I wasn't the type to change myself for a guy.

On Saturday afternoon he asked me to wear it again. I obliged, less enthusiastically this time.

And then he asked me something else.

I'd just finished dressing, reaching up to take the wig off. And he said behind me:

"Don't take it off."

I whipped around, my eyes narrowed. "What?"

"Sorry, I meant..." He paused, as if carefully wording what he was going to say next. "What if you didn't take the wig off right away? What if you wore it for a little longer? You know, cooking dinner, hanging out..."

Okay. This was too far.

"I'm not going to keep it on."

"Why not?"

I scowled at him. "For one, it smells. And it's uncomfortable. I don't like it."

I could see the look of disappointment on his face. I'll be honest, it hurt. What was wrong with my own hair? If he was so obsessed with blondes, why did he marry me? There were thousands of blonde women out there. Why not marry one of them, and forget the wig altogether?

"Can you just keep it on a *little* longer? You look so beautiful." He smiled at me. "It really just... becomes you."

I was really annoyed at this point. Like, seriously annoyed. But I was old enough to know that bargaining was a much more effective way to make both of us happy.

"I'll wear it if you make dinner. But as soon as we're done eating, I'm taking it off."

"Sure!" He grinned at me.

That stupid, big grin that I was really starting to hate.

Over the coming weeks, the "wig situation" escalated.

Almost every weekend Mark brought it out of the closet. Holding it in his hands tenderly, carefully, as if it were a delicate little kitten. "Want to wear the wig?" he'd always ask.

As if it were my idea.

I didn't want to wear it. But when I did, I noticed Mark did extra things for me. Cooking dinner. Doing the dishes. Buying me gifts. Slowly I began to just accept it. If wearing the thing got me out of chores, what did I have to lose? And besides, it wasn't such a big deal. I didn't wear spanx, or push-up bras, or lots of makeup.

Was a wig really worse than those?

I will say, though... it was weird how Mark seemed

against the idea of me bleaching my hair. I figured that would be a better, more permanent solution, but he was 100% against it. He threw out every reason in the book: *It's so expensive. And it takes so much upkeep. You'd have to do the roots every few weeks. And besides—the wig just becomes you.* I hated how he said that. *The wig becomes you.* Like the wig was becoming an appendage, a part of myself.

In the end, I don't know how I let it go on for as long as it did. I guess I just told myself it was a stupid fantasy that he'd get over sooner or later.

Boy, was I wrong.

I'd never seen a photo of Mark's first wife with hair.

The few photos on her memorialized Facebook page were after she'd started chemotherapy. She was either wearing a hat or a bandanna—never a wig, despite Mark's apparent obsession with them.

But one night I got curious about her. Curious if he pushed this weird stuff on her before the cancer. Did he make her dye her hair? Wear a wig? Or was she naturally blonde?

After an hour of poking around, I got my answer.

There was a wedding album in the attic, tucked away with some of Miranda's belongings and stuff from their life together.

Mark was out with some friends—he wouldn't be home for a few hours—but I still got a swoop of nervousness in my stomach as I pulled it onto my lap.

Our Wedding Album, it read in gold scrolling letters across the faux white leather cover.

And there—on the very first page—was my answer.

Miranda had the same hair as the wig.

I mean *exactly* the same. The same color—varied shades of gold. The same hairstyle—blown out with curtain bangs. It was identical.

Is she wearing the wig?

Or...

I didn't want to consider the second possibility.

Maybe, that was her natural hair. And he'd gotten an expensive, custom-made wig to look exactly like it. And he was making me wear it, so I'd look like her.

*So he could pretend I **am** her.*

The album fell out of my lap.

This can't be happening. He'd seemed so normal. Especially about his wife. Grieving but past it, the wound an old scar that had healed over. It'd been seven years since she died.

Apparently, I'd been dead wrong.

I picked the album back up and flipped through it for a little while. I studied her face, her scalp, looking for a seam. But the photos had that professional, airbrushed quality to them. If there had been any evidence it was a wig, the photographer cleaned it up in Photoshop.

I finally closed the album, went downstairs, and waited for Mark to get home.

I've never been one for subtlety.

By the time he got home I'd been stewing in my own thoughts for three hours. I'd brought the wig down and put it in the middle of the kitchen table. The blonde hair shone in the dim light, hanging limply of the faceless plastic stand.

Then I heard the jingle of keys—the click of a lock. His footsteps as he came towards the kitchen...

"You made me wear that wig so you can pretend I'm Miranda. Right?"

He froze in the doorway.

Yeah, that's right. I got you, you son-of-a-bitch. I slammed the album onto the kitchen table and pointed at the first picture. "Miranda's hair looks *exactly* like that wig."

His face went white. He opened his mouth and closed it a few times, as if trying to find the words. "You don't understand," he finally choked.

"Oh, I think I understand perfectly well. You're playing some sort of sick game, where you're trying to turn me into your dead wife."

He swallowed. Glanced behind him, as if afraid someone was crouching there, listening to us. Then he turned back to me, his voice lowered. "I only made a wig out of her hair because—"

"Wait." My stomach dropped as I parsed what he was saying. "Did you just say, *a wig out of her hair?*"

"I—"

"It's *her fucking hair?!*"

He sheepishly nodded.

I stared at the thing, my stomach roiling. Golden

strands hung limply off the wig holder, draping onto the table. *A dead woman's hair.* Of course. I should've known. It looked so beautiful, so real.

And that hair... had been *on* me. Bobby pinned to my head. Brushing against my shoulders. My *bare* shoulders. Fuck, I even pulled one from my nether regions the last time we had sex.

I felt sick.

"I'm leaving," I said quietly, shooting up from the table. I ran up the stairs and grabbed my overnight bag. Wildly grabbed clothes off the hanger, stuffed them inside. Grabbed my laptop, chargers—

His heavy footsteps thumped up the stairs.

And then he appeared in the doorway. A hulking shape dimly outlined by the kitchen light spilling upstairs.

"Leave me alone," I snapped, shoving my clothes in as fast as I could go.

Surprisingly, he didn't reply. No apologies, no pleading with me to stay. I ignored him and continued packing. Reached over and grabbed my Airpods from the bedside table, throwing them in. Then my phone—

Strong arms grabbed me from behind.

I screamed.

But it was no use. He was so strong. And then I felt it —something touching my head.

He was pressing the thick, stiff cap of the wig onto my head as he held me still. I heard his voice whispering something in a strange rhythm in my ear.

Then everything went black.

My hair is blonde.

I'm standing in the bathroom, admiring myself. There is a bloody seam at my scalp, but other than that, I look okay.

Mark comes up behind me and wraps his arms around my waist. "I love you so much," he says, kissing me tenderly on the cheek.

I forgive him for what he did. I understand everything now. Last night, I got up in the middle of the night and wrote it all out. Everything that happened before today. I had to get it out of my system. It was like a nightmare that kept replaying in my head, even though the bloody seam is evidence that it really did happen.

But now it's over.

Now, I'm who I was truly meant to become.

I comb a hand through my blonde hair. Then I turn to him and smile. "I love you, Mark," I say.

"I love you too, Miranda."

A little jab of *something* in my heart. Sadness? Should I feel sad that he's calling me her name? But I don't feel sad. Not really. I'm happy now.

I wrap my arms around him tighter—then pull him into a kiss.

FOOTPRINTS IN THE SNOW

I was in a bus crash with five other passengers.
After the crash, there were six.

—

All it took was a patch of black ice to send our Bluestar bus careening into a tree. I'd been trying to sleep. But between the guy snoring behind me, the jostling bumps, and the driver's radio, it wasn't gonna happen. *Twelve inches of snow expected... manhunt continues for Sterling inmate... heeeeere's the traffic report—*
CRUNCH.
My head smacked into the window.
Then everything went black.
When I opened my eyes, I was aware of only two things: the throbbing in my head, and the cold. My entire body was freezing, like I'd fallen asleep outside.
Where am I?

Oh, no...
I pushed myself up—
"Oh, you're awake, thank God." Harry rushed to my side, wrapping his arms around me. "Are you okay? How's your head?"
"It hurts," I groaned. "Is... is everyone okay?"
"Yeah. I mean, we're all scratched up and stuff, but... no one's seriously hurt."
I glanced around the bus. There was a teenage girl with blood running down her face, crying in her boyfriend's arms. An older lady who'd clearly had too many lip fillers, staring out the window with a glassy look. A white dude scrolling on his phone as if nothing happened, and a muscular bearded guy with a Jason Momoa vibe near the front.
"Did somebody call—"
"Yeah. But it's going to be hours," he said with a sigh. "The storm's gotten worse. They have to come up the mountain in a Snowcat."
"What time is it?"
"A little before three."
I pulled my coat on, zipping it up to my neck until it wouldn't go anymore. *It's so cold.* I had no idea how I was going to be able to stay here like this—head throbbing, body shivering—for hours. I looked out the windshield. The front of the bus was crumpled beyond recognition. It was a miracle the driver lived. And beyond the bus... The sky was deep gray, heavy with snow, as snowflakes steadily fell against the dark trees.
"Uh, everyone... we have a problem," the driver called from the front.

"No shit we have a problem!" the bearded guy snapped. "We're stranded here, with no food or water, in the middle of a blizzard. All because you weren't paying attention!"

"Hey, shut it. We all make mistakes. No one got hurt," Harry said next to me.

"Speak for yourself," the lip filler woman replied, rubbing her temple. "I think I have a concussion!"

"We're going to die out here," the teenage girl wailed.

"Quiet!" the driver screamed. And there was something in his voice—a note of panic—that set us all absolutely silent.

"Now, you listen to me very carefully," he said in a low voice. Barely above a whisper. "I drive this route all the time... and I know the woods around here are dangerous. It's just woods for miles and miles, and people see that as an opportunity. Hikers go missing. There's cult activity. I've seen it with my own two eyes—people throwing branches across the road to make you stop, but they're hiding in the bushes to ambush you." He paused, swallowed, and rubbed his hands together. "And I think we have, um... found ourselves in one of those types of situations."

"What... what are you talking about?" I stuttered.

The driver got out of his seat and walked towards the bus door, shards of windshield snapping under his feet. "Look."

Slowly, one-by-one, the seven of us got out of our seats. The doors were open, ice-cold wind whipping inside. *For fuck's sake. That's why it's so cold in here.* I opened my mouth to yell at the driver to close the door—

And then I saw it.

Footprints in the snow.

A single trail of them, leading from the darkness of the woods to the bus doors.

"Someone got on this bus *after* we crashed. Must've snuck in right after, when most of us were knocked out or trying to get our wounds fixed up." The driver lowered his voice to a whisper. "Someone is on the bus, right now. I don't know if they're hiding under the seats somewhere, or in the bathroom, or what. And I... I don't know what we should do. If we go into the woods, there might be more of them. But if we stay here, we might all die." His stern expression faded, and he sucked in a shuddering breath. "God, I've got a little three-year-old at home. I can't..."

He leaned against the crushed steering wheel, head in his hands.

The seven of us looked at each other. I squeezed Harry's hand, my heart pounding in my chest. *They probably just want our money. We'll hand over our wallets, and then the police will be here...*

This was supposed to be our second chance. One last shot at fixing our marriage, at finding what we'd lost. Now it felt like Fate was laughing at us. No way in hell you're getting a second chance.

"Lock the doors. It's eight against one," the angry bearded guy said, breaking the silence. "We can take 'im."

"What if he's got a gun, smartass?" the lip filler woman shot back.

"Kind of sexist to assume it's a guy," the phone dude said.

"I don't want to die," the teenage girl sobbed.

"Wait," he said. He looked up at us, his eyes wide in the darkness. "Oh. No, no, no."

"What is it?" I asked, a weight sinking in my chest.

"I only scanned six tickets." *One, two, three,* he mouthed, as he counted us again. "There—there are seven of you. But only six..." His face grew even paler. "Oh, God, it's—it's one of you."

What the fuck?

I looked at the other passengers, my heart pounding. But as my eyes settled on each of their faces, I honestly couldn't tell you whether they'd been riding with us or not. Teenage couple, lip filler woman, bearded guy, phone dude... I'd been trying to sleep most of the trip—and so had everybody else, I think. The interior lights had been off, and the bus was pretty dark.

The bearded guy straightened, towering over us. "So who is it, then? We'll play nice. Give you our wallets and everything. Just don't hurt us, and this will all play out smooth."

Silence.

"I think it's that guy," the lip filler woman said, pointing to the guy glued to his phone. "He doesn't look hurt."

"Dude? Seriously?" He looked up at us, and I could tell he was young, no more than 25. "My thumb is *fucked up*. I can barely text!"

The teenage girl locked eyes with me. Then she lifted a shaking finger—and pointed it right at me.

"You."

"What? You think *I'm* it?"

"No. I mean, I remember you." Her young, pretty features tightened into a scowl. "You were really rude. You literally *threw* your bag on top of mine. I have *designer* boots in here, and they might be crushed because *you* don't care about other people, and you probably don't even care if I die out here and—"

"Stop!" Harry shouted. "That's good, that you remember her. That's a fact that we can use. Does anyone else remember anyone else?"

"He was snoring behind me," the teenage boyfriend said, pointing at the bearded guy. "It was really annoying."

"Anyone else?"

Silence.

"Wait. Hang on. We can look everyone up on Facebook, can't we? Verify their identity?" I asked. I pulled out my phone—and my heart dropped. "Shit. No service."

"It's a miracle we got a call through the cops at all," the lip filler woman said.

I looked at the six other passengers. *Harry's my husband, so he's out. The teenage couple—they vouch for each other, don't they? Assuming the person isn't some memory-altering demon out of a horror movie.*

That left phone dude, bearded guy, and lip filler woman.

Three people.

One of them lying.

It was true that despite phone dude's protests, he was the least hurt of the three. He looked young and innocent, but you can't judge a book by its cover.

I looked at lip filler woman. Her face... her face was weird. That was the only way to describe it. I'd assumed it was the plastic surgery, but maybe not. There was something *off* about her whole eye area. And her face remained mostly expressionless this entire time...

Was it lots of Botox?

Or—could she be wearing a mask?

I stared at her neck, looking for a seam. But in the dim lighting, I couldn't make anything out.

Then there was bearded guy. He was intimidating. And he seemed like a ball of angry energy, ready to explode at any time. The blood on his sleeve didn't mean anything—there was blood everywhere. He could've just wiped some on to make it look good.

He seemed like the obvious choice, but then again, the teenager vouched for him.

"Maybe we should just go into the woods," I whispered to Harry. "Get away from everyone."

"You heard the driver. He said there might be more of them out there."

"But staying in here—"

"It's seven against one."

"But why aren't they *doing* anything yet? If they just wanted to rob us... they would've done it by now." I shuddered. "It's like they're *playing* with us."

"You can go out alone, if you want. But I'm staying here."

"I'm not going to—"

"Well, *I'm* not going to die because of your stupidity!"

There it was. The temper that had grown with each passing year of our marriage. I wanted to yell and scream at him, but I already knew that never worked. Instead I stared at the windshield, blinking away tears.

Small flakes flurried down, collecting in at the bottom of the windshield. Beyond was the stretch of road carving up the mountain, now pure white. The set of footprints leading out the door, their edges softened by the layer of fresh snow.

And... something else.

A lump. Just off the side of the road, at the border of the woods. Something about it caught my eye—even though, in the darkness and the snow, I couldn't make out any detail. It was like it didn't belong, like it clashed with the natural landscape.

And was that... a trail of footprints... leading up to it?

I narrowed my eyes, trying to parse what I was seeing. Had someone already left the bus? Gone out and come back? Was one of the passengers in on this whole thing?

And was that... *blood*... in the snow?

"Guys. Guys, look." I pointed out the windshield. My head throbbed as my heart began to pound, and I felt lightheaded. "Out there—there's a trail of blood—and something..."

The voices died down behind me. "Oh my God," the teenage girl whispered. Other mutters too—*what is that? Is that blood?*

Black spots danced in my eyes. I grabbed the driver's seat to keep my balance—

It was wet.

I pulled my hand away to see thick, red blood staining my fingers. *What...?* I looked down. The driver's seat was drenched in blood.

But the driver—

His clothes were dry.

No...

"It's the driver!" I screamed, backing away. *"It's him!"*

At first he didn't say anything.

Then he slowly turned around. And when I saw his face, my blood ran cold.

He was smiling.

Chaos erupted. I lunged for the door—but as soon as I stepped down, something yanked my arm back. My entire body jolted, my head screaming in pain. I whipped around to see the man, his fingers gripping me tight.

"Not so fast," he growled, his grin growing wider.

But then in a blur of color, Harry slugged him in the face. His grip loosened and I tumbled to the ground. Snow seared my skin, the ice cold burning my fingers, seeping through my pants.

Quickly the others raced out. The teenage couple, the woman, one of the guys. The bearded man joined Harry in trying to subdue the guy, trying to tackle him to the ground.

"Run!" Harry shouted, locking eyes with me. *"Run!"*

After a moment's hesitation, I ran. The others

followed, and we all ran deeper into the forest, terrified. We kept the road in our sight, and after a few hours of wandering, we spotted the lights of the Snowcat coming up the mountain.

As we ran, though, I couldn't stop thinking about what I'd heard on the radio. While I'd been trying to sleep. *Manhunt continues for Sterling inmate.*

Was that him?

By the time the police arrived, all three men were gone. They haven't been found. I'd like to think they're alive somewhere. That in a few days, Harry will come home. But I know, deep down, that's not the case.

The police did find the body of our real driver, though.

At the end of the bloody footprints in the snow.

THE SCARIEST
BOARD GAME

ZUCARI: THE SCARIEST BOARD GAME EVER MADE, read scrawling silver letters across a slim black box. It was my 21st birthday. My parents were out of town and I'd invited my two closest friends, Brianna and Elise, over to hang out. Brianna and I hadn't seen each other since she moved in with her boyfriend Dave, and Elise was constantly busy with her dozens of student clubs. So it was a rare moment to have the gang all together again. We'd been having a blast—making drinks, watching horror movies... and now opening presents.

"Looks creepy. Is it like *Betrayal at House on the Hill?*" I asked, sliding my fingernail into the seam and breaking the tape.

"Mmm, more like *Jumanji*," she replied, swallowing a sip of hard lemonade.

I pulled up the box lid. Inside was a folded board, a

deck of cards, a die, and a little baggie of metal game pieces. I slowly unfolded the board—and I had to admit, it was creepy. It depicted a dark forest with towering gnarled trees, and a path of game spaces that twisted and crossed and dead-ended.

"It's a pretty standard game. Roll a die. Go that many spaces. Draw a card. Do what the card says. And the game isn't over until someone reaches the cabin." Brianna pointed with a purple-lacquered nail to the drawing of a cabin in the far right corner of the board, windows glowing yellow.

I pulled the game pieces out one by one—metal spheres with a dot of colored paint on top. I took red, Elise took green, and Brianna took purple. We put all three on the 'START' square.

"Why don't you go first, birthday girl?" Brianna asked.

I took the die, shook it in my cupped hands, and let it fall. 3. I picked up my game piece and moved it three spaces--then reached for the deck and drew a card.

SOMEONE, OR SOME*THING*, IS WATCHING YOU. GO BACK TWO SPACES.

I lifted my arm to pick up the game piece--and paused.

"You okay, Cara?" Elise asked.

"Yeah. I just..." I turned around, looking towards the kitchen. I could've sworn... I don't know. It almost felt like a little gust of air on the back of my neck.

I smiled and shook my head. "You're up," I said, handing the die to Elise.

"Okay..." she said hesitantly, grabbing the die. 5. She moved her piece five spaces and then drew a card.

"It says, **YOU FIND WILD RASPBERRIES. GO FORWARD ONE SPACE.**"

Smiling, she advanced one space on the board—putting her marker in the middle of dark clearing with a small glistening pond. "You're up," I said to Brianna.

She rolled a 2. Drew a card, and read it out loud:

"**CLOUDS ROLL OVER THE MOON. TOO DARK TO SEE. LOSE A TURN.**"

At that exact moment, the lights flickered.

And then they went out.

"Welp. That was weird," Brianna said in the darkness.

"Was there supposed to be a storm tonight?" Elise asked, her voice tinged with fear. I felt her fingers find my hand in the darkness, then interlock with mine. "Or could... could someone have cut our power?"

"What, you mean, like a murderer?" Brianna asked, barely holding in a laugh.

"I don't hear any rain or wind or anything. And we *are* three girls, home alone..." She let out a breath. "Did we lock the doors?"

"Elise, it's okay," I said, giving her hand a reassuring squeeze. "We get power outages all the time. The wiring out here is shit. Does anyone have their phone? I left mine upstairs."

"Yeah, I got mine," Brianna said, rummaging in her pocket.

But before she could turn on her flashlight, I felt it.

A cool breeze. Wafting over my bare shoulders and through my hair. But the air was different—heavy, cool, damp. An earthy smell filled my nostrils, tinged with decay.

"Do you smell that?" I asked.

"Yeah. Smells like something died," Elise replied, sounding even more scared.

But before we could descend into a spiral of panic, white light flashed through the room. Everything was thrown into stark relief from the bright light of Brianna's flashlight. Black shadows stretched behind us, and our faces took on a sunken, creepy appearance, with black shadows sinking into every dimple, every line.

I looked down—and my breath caught in my throat.

Nobody was holding my hand.

Elise's hands were clasped tightly together in her lap.

"Elise... were you holding my hand? Just a minute ago?"

"No, why?"

"Brianna?"

She shook her head.

"You—this is a joke, right?" I scanned both of their faces, looking for a hint of a smile. "I felt someone holding my hand. This—this isn't funny, guys." My heart pounded in my chest and I sucked in a breath. Another breath of that damp, earthy air.

"We weren't holding your hand, okay? Geez. Chill out," Brianna said.

"*Somebody* was."

Elise's eyes went wide. "Maybe—maybe someone broke into the house—"

"You two are so easily scared it's ridiculous." Brianna rolled her eyes and handed the die to me. "Your turn."

I took it from her, a lump forming in my throat. *It had to be Brianna.* She liked to tease people, push their buttons. Exaggerate stories into tall tales, make herself the center of attention. Well, I wouldn't give her the satisfaction. I put on a brave face, grabbed the die, and rolled it. I moved my piece and then, slowly, plucked a card from the stack.

"**YOU FIND A LOST HIKER. GO BACK THREE SPACES,**" I read, confused. "Why would that be a bad thing?"

But then I heard it.

A soft shuffling sound, coming from the kitchen.

Every muscle in my body froze. "Did—did you hear that?" I whispered. Elise nodded at me, her dark eyes wide.

Slowly, I forced myself up.

I started walking towards the kitchen. It was almost pitch black; the light from Brianna's phone didn't quite reach. I forced my feet forward, until I was standing at the entrance of the kitchen.

I strained my ears to listen.

I thought all I would hear was silence. That the scuffling sound was just my imagination. But instead, I heard the soft, rhythmic rush of air.

Breathing.

"I'm calling the police!" I shouted.

The light behind me jittered. And then the kitchen lit up in dim tones of gray, as Brianna came up behind me with her flashlight.

I froze.

In the darkness, in the center of the kitchen, stood a man. He faced away from us, wearing hiking clothes. Something dark—like blood—covered his bare legs in patches.

My legs felt weak underneath me. I gripped the doorframe—

"Are you okay?"

I looked back to see Brianna and Elise behind me. But they didn't look scared. I whipped around—but now, the kitchen was empty.

"You—did you see—there was a man—"

"I didn't see anything," Elise said.

I ran through the house, Brianna and Elise behind me. But the doors were all still locked. I opened the pantry and looked under the sofa; there was no one down here. And I definitely hadn't heard anyone go up the stairs.

I guess... it had been dark. Maybe my brain interpreted some of the shapes and shadows of the kitchen as someone standing there. I *was* on edge. Brianna's prank had really messed with my head.

We finally sat back down at the game board. "Are you sure you want to keep playing?" Brianna asked.

I hated her tone. Like she was talking to a scared little child. "Of course I want to keep playing. Why wouldn't I?"

"You just seem a little... jumpy."

The dark, harsh shadows of her face scrunched into a smile. I grabbed the die off the board and handed it to Elise. "Your turn."

She glanced between us for a second, then hesitantly took the die. "One," she said, moving her green marker one space. Then she drew a card. "**WHILE TAKING A SWIM IN THE POND, YOU FEEL SOMETHING GRAB YOUR ANKLE. LOSE A TURN.**" Elise lifted her piece and moved it back. She started for the die—

Drip.

The three of us turned our heads to the foyer. *Drip.* A faucet was dripping—which sometimes happened when the power went out. Our well had an old electric pump that'd seen better days. "I'll get it," I said, hoisting myself up and walking into the dark foyer.

Brianna and Elise followed, the flashlight bouncing off the dark walls.

It didn't sound like it was coming from the kitchen, so I poked my head into the hall bathroom. Not there either. Which left only one option: my parents' bathroom. Their bedroom was the only one on the first floor.

I made my way into the dark hallway, Brianna and Elise following a few steps behind. The dripping grew louder. I swung the door to the bathroom open. *Drip, drip, drip.* It was coming from the bathtub.

I walked over, slowly, pulled the shower curtain back—

And froze.

The bathtub was full of water.

It glistened in the darkness, Brianna's flashlight reflecting on the water. "My... my mom must've forgotten to drain it," I said, staring down into the water. But I knew, deep down, that couldn't be right. My mom used all kinds of bath bombs and fragrant soaps. The water here was odorless, crystal clear.

I got on my knees and plunged my hand into the water, reaching for the stopper.

It was ice cold. I grimaced as I plunged my hand in further, reaching for the little ring on the stopper, curling my finger to hook into it. The cold felt like little knives across my skin, stabbing me everywhere. I reached deeper—

"No!"

Elise grabbed my shoulders and pulled me back.

I rolled back onto the tile, ice-cold water dripping down my arm, onto my shirt. "There—there was something in there," she panted. Her lips trembled as she stared at the bathtub.

"What the hell are you talking about?" Brianna asked.

"I saw something, okay?" Elise shot back, with a bite in her voice I'd never heard before. "Don't you dare tell me I didn't. There was something dark. Moving under the water. It looked like it was going right for Cara and I—"

"Okay. Okay." Brianna held up her hands in surrender. "I'm not going to fight you on it. Let's just go back into the family room, okay?"

She stepped over me, reached down, and quickly

pulled the stopper out of the bathtub. A little tornado appeared in the water, followed by the sound of water rushing and gurgling through the pipes. Then she stepped out of the bathroom.

Elise and I followed. But as I stepped out of the room... I could've sworn I heard a splash.

"I lost my turn with the whole moon thing, so it's Cara's turn again," Brianna said, sitting back down on the carpet in front of the board.

I sat down, eyeing Elise and Brianna hesitantly. Then I picked up the die and rolled it. Moved my game piece, picked a card off the stack and read it aloud.

"**WHILE HUNTING FOR FOOD, YOU HIT THE WRONG TARGET. LOSE A TURN.**"

SPLAT.

Something dark and wet fell onto the dead center of the board.

"What... what is that?" Brianna asked. For the first time, she sounded scared.

I slowly tilted my head and looked up.

There was a dark stain in the middle of the ceiling. With every second it grew larger. As if something upstairs, right above us, was quickly bleeding out into the floor.

I grabbed Elise and stared at the stain, too scared to move.

"We need to get out of here—"

Clack.

Brianna had already rolled her die. She grabbed a card; then it slipped out of her hands, falling onto the board and soaking into the blood.

"THE MUSHROOMS WERE POISONOUS. GO BACK TO START."

And then she began to retch. Horrible, choking coughs filled the room as she doubled over. She crawled forward across the carpet and began to vomit. "Call 911!" I screamed at Elise, as I grabbed her by the shoulders and tried to hold her up, try to keep her from choking on it.

Elise pulled out her phone. "There's no reception!" she cried, fingers frantically moving over the screen. *"No reception!"*

Brianna's body lurched in my arms as she threw up again. Vomit spilled over the carpet, threaded with blood.

And then she was still.

"Oh my God. Brianna? *Brianna?!*"

I grabbed her phone and started to dial 911, its flashlight bouncing all over the room. But Elise was right—the call didn't even connect. *No network.*

I motioned to Elise. Each of us put Brianna's arm over our shoulders and we began to hoist her up. "You're going to be okay," I said softly. "We're going to take you to the hospital—"

"We have to keep playing," she said weakly, bloodstained vomit dripping down her chin. "We have to... reach the cabin..."

"Okay, we'll keep playing," I said in a calm voice, exchanging a look with Elise. "But first we're just going to get you checked up—"

"*LISTEN TO ME!*" she screamed, her voice hoarse.

Elise and I froze.

"We have to keep playing. We have to reach the cabin." She tore away from us, breathing hard, wavering on unsteady feet. "This isn't just some game. Zucari is—it's fucked up. I only brought it here because Dave forced me to. He was going to—to hurt me if I didn't."

SPLAT.

Another drop of dark liquid splattered onto the game board.

"If we don't reach the cabin—if we don't finish the game—we all die."

She collapsed back down into the carpet, breathing hard. Then with a shaking, vomit-covered hand, she grabbed the die. "Cara... your turn." She held it out to me.

I paused, staring at the die.

Then I shook my head. "I don't know what the fuck is going on here, but I'm out." And with that, I turned on my heel and marched straight for the front door.

But it wouldn't open.

"What the fuck?"

I tugged at the door with all my might. It didn't budge. With a scream, I grabbed my mom's expensive vase off the front table and threw it at the window.

It shattered to a million pieces—but the window didn't even crack.

"Maybe... we should just finish the game."

I whirled around to see Elise standing behind me. She stared at me with wide, dark eyes. "Please, Cara," she whispered. "I don't want to die."

"We're not going to die. This is just some stupid prank—"

"Then why can't we open the door? Why can't we *call* anyone?!"

I looked at the door, my heart sinking.

Then I slowly walked back towards the family room.

The smell of decay had intensified. Damp, cold air clung to my skin. I stepped into the room and—*crunch*—something was under my feet. I looked down to see a few dried leaves, laying on top of the carpet.

And that's when I noticed the room was... different.

A pale, yellow moon hung outside the window—even though by this hour, it should have been high in the sky. A green lichen bloomed on the rough, gray upholstery of the sofa. The blind cords hung down to the floor like vines, and the mass of tangled cords that ran to the TV looked more like roots twisted around each other.

I swallowed and sat across from Brianna. Without a word, I took the die. Let it fall drew my card. I let out a sigh of relief.

"**YOU CROSS A STREAM AND STOP FOR A DRINK. GO FORWARD TWO SPACES.**"

I advanced my game piece, then handed the die—now coated in a thin layer of vomit and blood—to Elise. I could feel her hand shake shake as she took it from me.

Clack. Thwip.

Elise's eyes widened as she stared at the card. She opened her mouth—but no words came out. Just a horrible, choking sound.

And then I heard it.

A sound I've only ever heard once before in my life,

more than a decade ago. But filled me with absolute terror.

A soft, rattling sound.

Coming from the corner of the room.

Elise slowly turned her card around, and I saw the words: **RATTLESNAKE ATTACK. GO BACK TO START.**

A soft slithering sound echoed across the room. Elise scrambled back, climbing up onto the sofa. I glanced down at the carpet in the dim light, trying to pinpoint the snake's location.

But it wasn't carpet anymore.

Wet muck covered with decaying, damp leaves. Twisted roots and jagged rocks. The slithering sound grew louder and I froze, staring into the darkness, in the direction of the sound—

"Cara…" Brianna choked. "You have to finish the game."

I glanced at the board. I was seven spaces away from the cabin. Just a few more turns and I could make it to the cabin.

I snatched the die. It stuck to my fingers, staining my fingers red. I let it go and it tumbled across the painted trees.

3.

Shit. I'd have to roll a five or six to make it next turn.

I snatched the card from the top of the deck—and all the blood drained out of my face. **IT'S BEHIND YOU. GO BACK ONE SPACE.**

I immediately felt warm breath on the back of my neck. I squeezed my eyes tight, trying not to imagine what 'it' was. But I'd seen a shadow, in my peripheral

vision, stretching out behind me. A shadow with long, spindly arms—reaching out for me—
Sssshhhhh.
The rattling sound jolted me back into action. It was loud—only several feet away from me. Elise was crumpled into the couch, crying. Brianna was retching. I grabbed the die, shook it, and let it fall.
6.
Relief flooded me. I grabbed my red game piece and dropped it on the cabin. *Clack.* I looked up at Elise, shaking and staring at me; and Brianna, pale and trembling, lying on the floor.
But they were alive.
And there was only silence.

We never spoke of Zucari again.
Over the coming months Brianna, Elise, and I grew apart. After graduation, Elise went on to get her bachelor's. Brianna left Dave and got a job in the city. I stayed here, living with my parents as I continued at the IT company I'd been interning with.
But over the past few weeks, I've been seeing things.
Like a few days ago, I woke up in the middle of the night—and saw a man in bloodstained hiking clothes, facing away from me, standing still in my hallway.
Or when I took a bath to unwind from a particularly hard day at work—and felt something brush my ankle.
Or when I felt a gust of warm breath on the back of my neck as I made myself dinner.

And then there was last night. I woke up in the middle of the night, around 4 AM... and saw something outside that made my blood run cold.

A golden light, shining through the window of an old, abandoned cabin.

And what Brianna said echoed in my mind—

The game isn't over until you reach the cabin.

THERE'S SOMETHING IMITATING MY SON

"I thought you had him!"

"I thought *you* had him."

I glanced around the room, my heart pounding. "Danny?" I called. "Danny, where are you?"

Silence.

"Calm down. He's around here somewhere."

Our house wasn't even that big. Yet somehow, our six-year-old son was always disappearing. Sometimes I'd find him in one of the lower kitchen cabinets. 'Camping,' he called it, pretending the cabinet was his tent and one of his fake fire lanterns was the campfire. Other times I'd find him hiding in the closet, opening all his boxes of old toys and too-small clothing, throwing it all over the place just because.

"Okay, you search upstairs, I'll search down. DANNY!" I shouted.

"Geez, relax! He's probably just playing with his Legos. Or hiding in the closet again."

"Or drowning himself in the bathtub!"

My husband sighed, then started up the stairs. I went into full-on Mommy Panic Mode. I ran over to the family room—empty. Kitchen—empty. Then—

Fuck.

There he was.

Through the sliding glass door, I could see him. He was out in the yard. Or, at least, I saw his fake fire lantern. It bobbed up and down at the far end of the backyard. All the way down by the tree line.

How did he get down there so quickly?!

I threw the door open.

"DANNY!" I shouted. "GET BACK HERE, RIGHT NOW!"

The lantern stilled. Hanging just a few feet over the soft grass. I couldn't quite make out his small form, his little hand clutched over the lantern's handle.

"DANNY!"

He didn't move. *Dammit.* I burst out of the house, barefoot. My feet slid over the cold, wet grass. "DANNY!"

As I started gaining on him, he started moving. The lantern bobbed with each of his little steps. Getting further away from me.

Going into the woods.

"DANNY!"

"MIRANDA!"

I skidded to a stop. Turned around.

My husband poked his head out the back door. "Found him!" he shouted to me. "He's upstairs with his Legos."

I froze.

Looked back into the forest.

The lantern hung in the air, not ten feet away. The soft, fake firelight flickering. And beside it... a figure, that I could barely make out through the trees.

"What the..."

I turned around and high-tailed it back inside.

I ended up calling the police. The person holding the lantern was clearly too short to be an adult. What if a child had gotten lost and wandered into our yard?

They told me there were no missing children in the area—and a quick search brought up nothing in the woods, either. *Are you sure it was a kid?* they'd asked. And honestly, I couldn't tell them I was sure. It was a dark, moonless night. I'd only assumed it was Danny because of the lantern.

So I forgot about it, for a few days. But then, on Thursday night, I woke up around 2 AM to pee. And when I glanced out the window—

There it was.

Hovering just about ten feet from our back door.

"Kevin. Kevin, *wake up*," I said, shaking him. "There's someone out there."

I threw on my clothes and poked my head into Danny's room. Then I crept down the stairs, my heart pounding in my chest. Kevin followed behind. But when we got to the kitchen, the lantern light was no longer so close.

It was about halfway down our backyard, near the garden.

"It's back. That's what I was telling the police about," I whispered.

I watched as it floated in the darkness, just a few feet from the ground. Absolutely still.

Like it was *waiting*.

Waiting for me to follow it...

"Should we call the police?" I whispered.

Kevin gave a sigh. And even though he didn't say anything, I knew exactly what it meant. *You're overreacting again.* "This feels like a prank," he said, finally. "Some kid stealing our lanterns and taunting us."

"It... doesn't feel that way to me. What if it's a lost kid—"

"The cop said there weren't any kids missing in the area." He reached for the door. "I'll just go out there and tell them off."

"You can't go out there."

"Why not? It's just a kid."

I bit my lip as he slid the door open and walked out into the night.

I watched his shadow walk into the yard, then stop. "Hey! You," he called out. "I'm going to call your parents and tell them you're out here."

Silence.

"You hear me? Get out of here!"

The light bobbed.

And then it started coming *towards* him.

My blood turned to ice. I wrenched open the door. "Kevin! Kevin, *get in here!*"

For a moment, he hesitated.

Then he turned around and ran as fast as he could.

As soon as he got inside, he slid the door closed with all his might. Locked it. Yanked the string to make the blinds cover it.

"It—it's not a kid," he whispered.

My breath caught in my throat. I immediately imagined some horrible monster, some Gollum-like creature crawling around our yard with our lantern.

But what my husband said was far, *far* worse.

"It's a man," he said, barely able to catch his breath. His wide eyes locked on mine, and I could see the terror in them.

"It's a man... walking around on all fours... holding the lantern in his mouth."

The nightmares continue in...

AVAILABLE NOW

My wife and I have been playing hide and seek for three days straight.

I babysat a parrot. It said some... disturbing... things.

The same man is appearing behind my friends on Zoom. But we live hundreds of miles apart.

The light switches in my house are on the wrong walls.

DON'T LOOK brings you 30 terrifying tales for your darkest nights. This collection has every flavor of horror, from terrifying spectres to strange medications, from haunted farms to sinister games. Read... if you dare.

Hungry for more horror? Visit www.blairdaniels.com or sign up for my newsletter.

Thanks for reading!

Printed in Great Britain
by Amazon